D0485992

The
Trick
of It

By the same author

THE TIN MEN
THE RUSSIAN INTERPRETER
TOWARDS THE END OF THE MORNING
A VERY PRIVATE LIFE
SWEET DREAMS
*
CONSTRUCTIONS
*
PLAYS I
*
CHEKHOV: PLAYS
(*translation*)
*
THE ORIGINAL MICHAEL FRAYN
(*collected journalism*)

The
Trick
of It

MICHAEL FRAYN

PICADOR USA

A METROPOLITAN BOOK

HENRY HOLT AND COMPANY

NEW YORK

THE TRICK OF IT. Copyright © 1989 by Michael Frayn. All rights reserved. Printed in the United States of America. No part of this book may be used or reproduced in any manner whatsoever without written permission except in the case of brief quotations embodied in critical articles or reviews. For information, address Picador USA, 175 Fifth Avenue, New York, N.Y. 10010.

www.picadorusa.com

Picador ® is a U.S. registered trademark and is used by
Henry Holt and Company under license from Pan Books Limited.

For information on Picador USA Reading Group Guides, as well as ordering, please contact the Trade Marketing department at St. Martin's Press.
Phone: 1-800-221-7945 extension 763
Fax: 212-677-7456
E-mail: trademarketing@stmartins.com

A portion of this book first appeared in *The New Yorker*.

Library of Congress Cataloging-in-Publication Data

Frayn, Michael.
    The trick of it / Michael Frayn.
        p. cm.
    ISBN 0-312-42144-3
    I. Title.

PR6056.R3T75 1989
823'.914—dc20   89-40430

First published in the United States by Viking Penguin,
a division of Penguin Books USA

First Picador USA Edition: December 2002

10 9 8 7 6 5 4 3 2 1

S HE'S COMING.

I told you I made three attempts to get her to lecture, and she wouldn't. Wouldn't, she said, couldn't – never lectured. But then I had this sudden inspiration – how do these things come to one? – and dashed off a note (in my own hand this time, which is perhaps what did the trick, because as all the world knows she always writes by hand herself) saying could my students talk to *her*? Adding how her book had made them question some of their most fundamental whichwhats and indeed set off the most extraordinary ferment of intellectual whatever. It'll end up with her talking to them, naturally, so we're all happy.

Now of course I can't help asking myself why? Why is she coming? What's in it for her? She must know what it's going to be like. No one to meet her at the station. (Well, in this case there *will* be, of course – there'll be me, with flowers in my hand and the complete biography in my brain – but how's she to know that?) A grim little

5

gathering in my rooms, with half the students dumbstruck and the other half patronizing, then dinner with a handful of academics in unsympathetic disciplines who'll pretend they don't know who she is, then a night in some bleak guest room in a windswept corner of the campus, and then no one to tell her where to find breakfast.

I mean would you? Should I? Well, of course we should – we do it all the time. That's us. That's our dreary trade. But should we if we were her?

I also can't help asking myself what's in it for me? Of course, I shall take the opportunity to try out my theories about the superstitious dog in the first chapter of *TSR*, and the psychic lemur at the end of *FDDS*, and to find out whether KG and the boy in *Scatterbrain* are based on DB and her son (cf., if you've forgotten who DB is, my letter to you approx. MDLXIX in what will surely one day be my *Collected Correspondence*), and, just possibly, rather late in the evening over the brandy-glasses, whether the Palace of Long Afternoons in *TSR* is in any way autobiographical, and why things in her books are always catching fire (even in *WW*, which I always think of as a relatively uneventful sort of book, the family refrigerator suddenly bursts rather porten-tously into flames for no very good electrical reason). But do I really want to be told the answers? Isn't it cheating? Won't it take all the fun out of my researches?

I suppose she just wants a little trip. A day off. Someone else doing the cooking and deciding what to talk about.

I don't think I want to meet her at all. I expect my

rivals in the field all know her personally, but that's no concern of mine. I don't know why I call them rivals. That's not how I think of them. Fellow-specialists. Comrades in arms. I expect my esteemed colleague Vlad the Impaler is always masterfully sweeping his specimens off on joint family holidays in Tuscany before he puts them into the killing-bottle and pins them into his collection. And I'm sure that creepy little woman from somewhere in Pennsylvania who can't spell heuristic, Dr Stoff, or Swoff, or whatever she's called, is over here every summer with little jars of home-made arse-salve, weasling her way in to dinner. I always thought we in Britain were above such things. Or rather, I never thought anything at all. The idea of trying to scrape an acquaintance with her has never crossed my mind. Could this just be lack of imagination? Or is some unconscious resistance at work here? And doesn't the unconscious have its reasons that reason knows nothing of? All these years of quiet scholarship, and suddenly I'm careering off the rails. (Not just five years of *TBAD*. Do you know I was teaching *TSR* and *FDDS* at that summer school I did in Ontario *eleven* years ago?) Maybe the sight of her there at the station in all her circumstantiality – I mean, in an x-coloured coat and y-coloured shoes, z inches shorter than me – will destroy the magic. I shake her hand, and feel not the virtue in her flowing into me, but the virtue in me leaking away into her! Flesh! We're not into flesh, in our trade. So then how do I teach on, magic-less, to the end of the term – the end of the year – the end of my career?

I say z inches shorter than me. z = 5. I've just looked

in my notes. Oh God, there's going to be nothing but disappointment in meeting someone you know everything about already. There's something I don't know? Then I know where to look it up. I know her mind and I know her heart, and I know them backwards, forwards and sideways. I know them better than she knows them herself. I know what she looks like. I know what she looked like when she was twelve and when she was seventeen. Seeing her in her x-coloured coat and y-coloured shoes is just going to reduce her to a single set of arbitrary particulars.

I can't bear the thought of introducing her to people. There is no way of saying, 'And this is . . .' (I can't bear even to say it to you) without sounding either overawed or altogether too casual. In fact I shall introduce her not as J L but as Mrs M. I shall introduce her as Mrs M because, in the eyes of God, Mrs M is her name. Not many people know this, apart from me and (I assume) you and (I think) God. I usually call her Mrs M to myself. When I have to refer to her in my thoughts, in the course of formulating some professional judgement. 'A thread of residual Manichaeanism,' I think to myself, 'runs like a seam of black coal through the complex geology of Mrs M.' I am too scrupulous to drop her name even to myself, you see. So I certainly don't want to go littering the floor of the Faculty Dining Room with it. We like to keep the place reasonably clean.

But then I can't go round saying 'And this is Mrs M,' when even the least literate halfwit in Applied Cryogenics can see that in fact it's *her*.

What you may not know is that Mr M was a rare-book dealer. He made himself as scarce as his books, to turn a bit of a phrase, some years ago. Well, fourteen years ago. But who's counting? Only God and me, probably. He was five foot ten and a half, I should perhaps inform you.

I know everything, you see. Well, 'five foot ten and a half' is a slight liberty, a little *jeu d'esprit*. A plausible invention. What one might call taking a leaf out of the opposition's books. Because that's what these people do. Did you know that? They make things up. Off the top of their heads. *Pour un oui ou un non.* Piff paff. And then honest working folk like us, in our great concrete knowledge factories, have to *report*, have to *learn*, have to *know*, have to *expound* these shrugged-off nothingnesses. Ain't it all a blooming shame?

I realize now, now that I've said it – and I mean now, between the last paragraph and this – that I am serious about my second thoughts. But I mean *seriously* serious. I absolutely do not wish to meet this woman.

Well, this must seem all very ridiculous to you in the sunshine out there. I don't suppose you've ever got into these difficulties with your friend Mr Goethe, have you? But she is good, you know, my Mrs M. That's the maddening thing. She can do it, whatever it is that these people do. The closer I've looked for these eleven years, the better I've thought she did it. And the less I've understood what it is the buggers do.

Oh God, how would you like it if you heard that your Mr G was on Qantas even now, and you knew you had to meet him at the airport and show him Melbourne and ask him a few not entirely idiotic questions about the composition of *Faust* and the language of *Elective Affinities*? And go on teaching him for the rest of your life?

Now I've got to break it to the student body that they're going to meet her – that they are longing to meet her.

I shall report anon. You are keeping these letters, aren't you? You are storing them in steel filing-cabinets guaranteed proof against white ants and bush fires? They may, in years to come, turn out to constitute my entire literary remains; they may prove to be the text of my long-awaited *JL: A Critical Study*.

What's happening to you, by the way? In your last letter, I seem to remember, you were knee-deep in some steaming relationship which occupied almost the whole of every Thursday afternoon. By my calculation this is your seventh sultry saga since you arrived in Australia. Is the population of the country large enough to support depredations on this scale for much longer? They always seem to end up in tearful scenes in parked cars. Why don't you concentrate on arranging proper entertainment for your students, like me?

Funny occasion. *Funny* occasion! I mean the visitation from the subject of my studies.

First thing to report: she is *absolutely ordinary*.

Let us define our critical vocabulary. I mean that, were you to introduce her to your genteel but semi-literate family, or I to my semi-genteel and quarter-literate one, they would not raise an eyebrow. She is quietly spoken, slightly plumper than I expected from the photographs, almost motherly. She didn't want to talk about books, least of all hers, and when forced to by some of my more obstreperous over-achievers, she seemed slightly perplexed, as if she had found these volumes with her name on the title-page lying on her bookshelves one day and couldn't quite account for their presence. And what she said about them had a wonderful dullness and brownness, like the linoleum in some old-fashioned public library. She said it was important to make the reader feel at home in a book. She said she had found it was no good trying to write about characters she didn't respect. You should allow yourself no more than one major and one minor coincidence per book. Etcetera. If the Faculty Board had heard such things on my lips I should certainly find myself looking for other employment in the coming academic year, probably as an encyclopaedia salesman. But coming from her, of course, they had a most impressive air of gnarled integrity, of hard-won simplicity.

I could see that some of my more serious students, particularly my Female Foucault from Flixwich, were looking a little shaken by all this, as if Moses had held up the tablets of stone and they had nothing on them but the by-laws of the Mount Sinai National Park. But I was charmed. I quietly shelved all my plans to ask her about fire-symbolism, whether KG was really DB, etc., and asked her about her favourite authors instead, which I think was the right move, though favourite television programmes might have been better still. (If I tell you that joint *third* on the hit parade were the Brothers Grimm, there are ten points to be won for naming me numbers one and two.) And everybody in the Faculty Dining Room afterwards was very impressed. The Bald Eagle put his head a little on one side as he chewed, and watched her silently with those impassive, predatory eyes. The good Pope John himself beamed and chuckled and raised his hand in blessing. They all knew who she was, of course, though she is disconcertingly more mobile and alive than you'd guess from still photographs. Even the women thought she was wonderful. Or at any rate this is what La Beldam Sans Merci whispered to me over the Returned Trays. 'Isn't she wonderful?' said the

Beldam, with that dreadful little grin she has, and that dreadful little flickering of the eyelids. And for once the Beldam was right. Wonderful is *precisely* what she is. Like the Queen.

The Queen! Yes! That's what she's like! Or rather, she's what the Queen would be like if the Queen were less like the Queen. I mean, if she didn't talk in a funny voice, if she wrote books or taught the Romantics, like everyone else. She has that same maddening air of being quietly and unshakeably right, of being absolutely who she is, and of considering this an entirely sufficient explanation for her presence in the world. She is *our* Queen – by the Grace of God Defender of the Fiction, Empress of Character and Sovereign of the Blessed Plot.

I mock, but only the better to express my awe. Because in our age of doubt and relativism, the survival of such a stable literary monarchy, such *wonderfulness*, must be the envy of the world. No, but it is rather surprising. Don't you think? Did I say earlier that she was *ordinary*? I see, on examining the record (Richard Dunnett, *Collected Correspondence*, p. 4003), that I did. *Absolutely* ordinary was the phrase I used. Let me modify this a little. She is *absolutely extraordinary*.

I think she is at peace with herself. (A sudden shift of authorial tone here towards the reverential, placing no doubt considerable strain on the reader's flexibility of response.) Even in my sheltered life I have met authors before, as you know, and they seemed to me insecure creatures, childishly eager for approval and reassurance, much given to queasy philosophies of love for all mankind except, naturally, critics and fellow authors. (Well, you know who I have in mind.) So to see this simple monarch, this . . . this *woman*, sitting with such modest dignity amidst my students and colleagues, talking to the former about how to find a good literary agent, and to the latter about gardening and cats, touched my heart most strangely. She talks, I should say, quietly and sparingly. And she listens when other people talk. She has a certain way of looking at you while you're talking . . . Well, she doesn't blink. That's it. It's taken me all this time to think what it is that's so striking about that look of hers. You talk, and she looks at you with those thoughtful eyes (hazel, if you like to know these things), and she doesn't blink or look away, so you find yourself saying rather more than you intended. And no doubt she's making a mental note of it all (isn't this what writers do? – as if some kind of mental Pitman's were squiggling across their brains), and planning to put you into her next book – but let her, let her! I can think of no happier fate than to be lured in through those ever-open doors, taken to pieces inside that well-concealed brain, cleaned up, re-designed, made credible, given a function in some properly organized plot, and then reborn through those motherly fingers; to become ink (blue, Swan) emerging from the nib (gold, 18-carat) of her pen (black, Water-man's); and to be laid out (on the luxurious hundred-gram Conqueror bond she always uses) beneath the eyes of all literate mankind and all eternity. You see what I mean about her being the Queen.

I suppose I did indeed talk rather a lot. Not at dinner.

At dinner I sat in silence like a proud owner, watching everyone else as they first tiptoed admiringly round her, then succumbed and talked about not just gardening and cats but their childhoods and their parents. In the Common Room afterwards, though, I got her to myself, and I told her all about – well – yes – my childhood and my family. About my mother and my Auntie Annie, and Ted and June, and Griffins the newsagents. I've told you all about them, too, so don't look like that – and I've actually taken you into Griffins, but of course you've forgotten. It was where I spent my childish pennies, with odious piety but touching wrongheadedness, on *Books and Bookmen*. You remember now? Or are you looking like that because you're jealous? My God, this is the woman I have devoted the last twelve years of my life to! Alone together at last. Naturally I had to tell her things. Though now it occurs to me that the look on your face is not jealousy at all – it's professional surprise that I was telling her all about *my* mother and aunts when I should have been asking her about *hers*, not to mention the identity of DB and the possibility of spontaneous combustion in refrigerators. Yes. Well. What can I say? You're right. But I blink when I talk and she doesn't. If I could look straight into people's souls then people would be teaching me and babbling to me about their tedious adolescent awakenings in one of the few remaining cities that no one has ever written about. And I should be writing about this unfortunate place, and putting it at last on the literary map.

I have to confess, though, that I went on talking even

when the X-ray equipment was no longer focused on me. I mean when I was walking side by side with her under the uncertain streetlighting in the remoter parts of the campus, escorting her back to one of our grim but serviceable guest rooms at the end of this remarkable evening. By this time I was telling her – this is too shameful – about my views, so dear and familiar to you, on the mathematical representation of narrative time-scale, and she was listening as intently as ever, and smiling as warmly. Smiling? you query keenly. How do I know she was smiling when we were walking shoulder to shoulder, our eyes unable to leave the dim concrete pathway ahead for fear of stumbling over something hard, or stepping into something soft? – Because I could feel the smile on my shoulder, through the sleeve of my jacket. The warmth of it, you see. I did mention her smile? Perhaps I didn't. I was thinking about her eyes. But beneath the eyes, extending the look in them by other means, the smile. And the smile had light, of course, but also warmth. Like the sunshine that brings forth the tender buds in May. Like deep-heat treatment with ultra-short radio waves. Have you ever had it? I had it for my shoulder last year, after the window fell on it. You can't see anything, you can't feel anything on your skin. But there is a sense of internal well-being. It was the same sensation exactly as we walked past Low-Temperature Physics and the hockey pitches. In the same shoulder.

So that was my visitation from the Muse, my brush with the divine fire. A brief handshake at her door, another of the smiles and I was walking back to my own rooms. And in the nick of time, you murmur coldly. Any further exposure to this particular sunshine, and the patches of strange pigmentation on my prose style would have begun to spread uncontrollably. And yes, I was a little shaken, I have to confess, as I turned out of Rutherford Way into Joliot-Curie Circle, and the late autumn wind set the old newspapers dancing in front of Human Disciplines. Should I bring the same dispassionate eye as before to her work, which after all was *my* work? I have in the past (as you know) had reservations about some aspects of the *oeuvre*. But, as I strode along Dirac Drive, and the milkman rattled his bottles outside Machine Intelligence, I couldn't remember what they were. A bad sign. I will write a long letter to my old mucker in Melbourne, I thought, and kill two birds with one tome. I'll get it all off my chest (does this poor exhausted metaphor refer to some mysterious weight pressing on the outside or to bronchitic lungs full of phlegm within?) and at the same time relieve the dreariness of his Australian exile by providing an opportunity for jealousy, irritation, disapproval and condescension. So here we are, off my chest and on to yours – a great gob of narrative phlegm, spat ten thousand miles down the airways by your fellow-toiler in the vineyard of knowledge, R.

Hold on, though, you think. Don't put this letter in the envelope just yet. Write a P, you urge me, and then an S. Let's discuss this a little further. Because, with your usual acute eye for the text, you have noticed a tiny discrepancy in the account above.

Milk bottles. The clashing of, by milkman outside Machine Intelligence. Do we sit *that* long over the port at this ancient university? you ask. Or was that brief handshake at the door of the guest room not quite so brief after all?

Well. All right. Yes. There is no great lingering over the *digestifs* here, if only because the Senior Common Room is locked up for the night by eleven-thirty, as you probably remember. The phrase 'brief handshake', it's true, doesn't fully cover the events outside the guest-room door. They were extended by one of those odd little things that are so difficult to give any account of afterwards – the kind of snaggle in the narrative that you leave out when you tell the story.

You wait, gravely.

No, no, no. Not like that at all.

I stopped, when we had got to within some two to three yards of the guest-room door, and said 'Well . . .' in a valedictory and regretful tone, which I think you will agree is the usual way of approaching the end of an evening. She stopped and replied in similar style. (I think her actual words were 'Yes, well . . .') I took her hand. I thanked her for coming. She thanked me for inviting her. Nothing odd so far, of course. If the conversation had ended at that point I should have been passing Machine Intelligence in Dirac Drive some seven hours before the milkman got there. But then she said: 'I'd ask you in for a drink, only of course there's nothing to drink.' Still not too surprising. But then I said: 'Oh, as a matter of fact I put a bottle of whisky on your dressing-table for you, just in case you felt like a nightcap when you got back.' A little surprising? Mildly surprising, I think. I don't make a habit of supplying visiting lecturers with private bottles of Scotch, I can assure you. (Did you find one on *your* dressing-table when you came and gave us your thoughts on Mörike, the Middle Years?) It certainly took her a little aback, anyway, because there was a perceptible pause before she replied, which must account for a little of the missing time, though not, I should guess, for more than three or four seconds of it. Then she smiled, which I suppose accounts for another couple of seconds. And then she said: 'Come in.'

I see an eyebrow moving a fraction of an inch further away from me beneath my feet down there in Melbourne. Wait, though – we haven't got to the really odd bit yet. The really odd bit was that when she had unlocked her room and we went inside there was no whisky on the dressing-table. It had vanished.

Well, things are always vanishing from rooms. Radios, complete stereo-systems. The disappearance of the odd bottle of whisky is no great mystery. But I could see, from the way she smiled at me, that she didn't believe I'd ever put it there in the first place. Now, here's the weird thing. This is the snaggle in the narrative. Nor did I.

I suddenly couldn't remember putting it there. I could remember remembering it. That's to say, I could remember that when I had said, outside the door, that I had put a bottle of whisky on her dressing-table, it was because I remembered putting a bottle of whisky on her dressing-table. But now a terrible suspicion came to me. What I had remembered was perhaps not putting the whisky there at all, but *imagining* putting it there. A passing fantasy had somehow lost its label inside my head, and been filed with remembered events.

Well, as you can imagine I was very shaken. In my professional confidence, first of all. To her it matters not at all whether an actual refrigerator in the external world once burst into flames, or whether the event happened only inside her imagination. Or, for that matter, whether she thinks she remembers it even though she in fact invented it, or whether she thinks she invented it when in actual fact it really happened. Why should she care, if it makes the effect she intends? But to us, to you and me, these fine distinctions are vital. They are the essence of our trade. Just as the refrigerator repair-man must know what sort it is, whether a Frigidaire or an Electrolux, so we must know whether it was a real refrigerator or an imaginary one, or one that was converted in the imagination from a real television set, say, or whether it was a real refrigerator that had burst into imaginary flames. And we must know that we know. And know that we know that we know.

I was also shaken because she could see that I was shaken. As I stood looking, shaken, at the empty dressing-table, I caught sight of her reflection in the mirror, and her reflection was not looking for the whisky. It was looking at me and smiling. It seemed to me that she (or her reflection) had understood only too clearly about my little confusion of fact and fiction. She may even have found it somewhat suggestive that I had got my trade mixed up with hers, as if our hair, say, or our feet had suddenly become curiously entangled.

So, an odd moment, certainly, but was it worth describing it? It led nowhere, a meaningless eddy in the current of events. Since there was nothing in the room to drink, there was, *ipso facto*, no drink for this little episode to lead to. Well, there was water in the taps at the hand-basin in the corner. And this, in fact, is what we resorted to. She went silently to the basin, poured a glass of water and offered it to me. I drank it in silence (obviously). She watched me in silence. Thoughtfully. When I had finished she refilled the glass and drank a little water herself. (There was only one glass.) I silently watched her in my turn. (In my case because I couldn't think of anything to say.) After a while she sat down on the edge of the bed and looked thoughtfully at the floor. The floor interested her at least as much as I did. She took another sip, and then she held out the glass to me. I sat down beside her on the edge of the bed (there was nowhere else to sit) and took a sip. I gave her the glass. She sipped. She handed the glass to me. I sipped.

I to her. Sip.

She to me. Sip.

The glass was empty. I turned to her. We had now been silent for a number of minutes, and it seemed to me high time that one of us said something. I was not sure what words would come out. Perhaps something about the flaming refrigerator or the psychic lemur at last. Or perhaps just, 'The glass is empty.' But I said nothing. She was smiling again, and her lips were gleaming wet from the water. This is why I kissed them, because there was water on them and the glass was dry.

– Hold on a moment, I can imagine you saying at this point.

What is it?

– On a point of academic interest. This descent upon her lips is merely one single move in a whole campaign. What interests the outside world, surely, is not the tactics but the strategy. At what point did you actually decide on this course of action?

What course of action?

– Making a pass at her?

The dismissive coarseness of your expression is inappropriate. I was not making a pass. I know what passes are. I have made passes. I have had passes made at me. I have described some of these passes to you in earlier letters. This was not a pass. This was mutual. Nor did I decide. I knew. We both knew. She knew that I knew and I knew that she knew.

– When?

What?

– When did you know?

I'll tell you. We knew as soon as I met her at the station. I stepped forward as she walked down the platform and I smiled. She smiled. I took her hand and introduced myself. She looked at me, and there was the faintest suggestion of speculation in that look. Perhaps because it went on for a fraction of a micro-second too long. So then I knew. And she knew that I knew. And I knew that she knew that I knew. And she —

– Yes, yes, yes (you interrupt). But what about the bottle?

What?

– The bottle of whisky. Are you telling me you put it into her room, or imagined that you might put it into her room, or whatever you or your unconscious did or didn't do, *after* you met her? When she was already occupying the room?

Obviously not. I imagined putting the bottle of whisky into her room when I collected the key from Administration.

– Before you went to meet her at the station?

Naturally. But that was merely something that flashed into my mind and vanished again. A possibility. One has to be prepared for every eventuality. I assume you have insurance against various remote catastrophes. That doesn't mean you *expect* your snug little home to be consumed by bush fires or white ants.

– The Durex Fetherlite. Were they a further insurance against natural disasters?

What are you talking about?

– The three Durex Fetherlite you bought. Don't raise your eyebrows in some ridiculous attempt at denial. Everybody in the world knows by now. You bought them from the machine in the bogs at the Students Union, after all. A member of the faculty running into the Union, changing a fiver for five ones from the secretary of Rag Week, then rushing excitedly into the gents – what do you think they thought?

I have long campaigned for a machine in the Senior Common Room for precisely such emergencies.

– This was an emergency?

Not exactly. But there had been fire-hazard warnings. White ants had been seen on the march. It seemed prudent to take out an additional policy.

– This was *after* you'd met her at the station?

Exactly. Look, I had ten minutes between the seminar and dinner . . .

– Because you knew that she knew that you knew that –?

That was a figure of speech. No one can know another's knowledge. Because I speculated that she speculated. Look, on second thoughts I may not send this letter after all. Don't be offended. I don't mind a little gentle ribbing. After all, I've never kept anything back from you in the past. I told you every detail of my embarrassments with Rosie G and my recent ennuis with my rather persistent little chum in Anglo-Saxon Studies – even my amazing idyll with the lady from Tuscarora. I told you about the time I choked on the absent-mindedly chewed-off corner of a Barclaycard sales-voucher at the Vice-Chancellor's enstoolment, and the terrible night I was caught short behind the cyclotron. I don't mind your spying on me in the bogs, or crashing in on me when I'm in the middle of kissing someone, not even when the lady I'm kissing is old enough to be my, well, my former Director of Studies. But these soft bulges beneath my hand were not just parts of a woman – they were bits of an author, of (as I believe) a very fine author, just possibly of a great author – of an author whose works I had been reading and studying and expounding for the past twelve years! This sheer jut of the right hip, which I could feel beneath my hand now, was an outrage against public decency which no decent member of the public could be expected to resist – but the outrage was being committed by the last leg of a literature course that begins with the *Mabinogion*!

No, I shall certainly not post this letter. Now I know that you will never read it I can be completely frank. Because the terrible truth is this. It seemed to me, even as I broke it, that I had discovered a new taboo governing mankind, one which must have existed unknown since the dawn of time until I stumbled upon it yesterday evening – a taboo against intercourse with an author on your own reading-list. New to me, at any rate. I never heard lewd references to it in the changing-rooms at school, not even from Tony Gleat, who made obscene reference to the charms of his own and other people's mothers. I have never come across it in Sophocles or the *News of the World*. This is worse than the love that dare not speak its name; this is the love that doesn't even have a name to speak. Somewhere in common or statute law there must be a distant parallel; illicit sexual relations with a reigning monarch, perhaps. Is it a taboo that you have ever come across? You have probably considered it no more than I ever did. Less, in fact, since your chances of sharing a glass of water late at night on a narrow guest-room bed with Goethe or Mörike down there in Melbourne are so remote. But when you think about it (as you suddenly are at this present moment, surely), when you think of your hand (yes, *that* hand, it doesn't

matter which – either of the hands with which you were
so recently typing Goethe's name in reverential tones) –
feeling the irresistible smoothness of his knee . . . now
sliding under his skirt . . . now reaching the lace trimming
along the edge of his knickers . . . then at once you feel
(am I right?) the authentic shock of sheer moral horror.

One's sense of outraging a divine sanction is made
more acute (don't you feel, now that you find yourself in
your imagination alongside me on the bed?) because
one's desire contains an element of frankly professional
interest. Unwrapping this particular parcel is what one is
paid to do, after all. Patiently, over long years, using
nothing but one's native intelligence and sensibility, plus
a set of pink file cards and a little Olympia portable given
one by one's parents as a graduation present, one has
unpicked the knots, folded away the sheets of brown
paper for use next Christmas, lifted boxes out of packing.
Now, suddenly, one has only to undo a button here and a
hook there, and gently slide back the innermost wrapping,
to get to the very heart of the mystery, to discover things
that one never guessed one would know in one's lifetime,
never knew that one *wished* to know . . .

And now almost wishes one didn't know. I know, for
instance, that . . . No, this is something I can't tell even
you.

Though since I've definitely decided not to send you
this letter, I suppose . . . No. Sorry.

– Oh, come on, you say. (Or would say, if you'd got
this letter.) It won't shock *me*, you assure me.

Well, it *should* shock you!

–All right, you say, it *will* shock me.

Very well, then. You need a bit of a shock. Listen: I know that her underwear dsntmtch.

– What? you cry uncomprehendingly.

What do you mean, what? Why are you shouting 'What?' like that at me if you didn't get this letter? In any case I'm not going to say it any louder than that. Dsnmtch. OK? *Dsntmtch*! Oh, come on! Use your brains! No? I'll write it down and wrap it up in three pairs of brackets, then.

([〈doesn't match〉])

There. I've said it. Her underwear doesn't match. That is how she is now fixed in the annals of scholarly inquiry. With white knickers and peach bra. Not, of course, that I intend to include this fact in my lectures. Not that I am thinking of even letting it drop in private conversation with my post-graduate students. But it will be there at the back of my mind as I re-read *TBAD*. It will inform my perception of the novels.

If only she could have been wearing white with white! Or even peach with peach. I suppose it could have been worse. It could have been peach bra and lime-green knickers. I don't think I could have borne that. I think I should have struck her off the reading-list at the end of this academic year and taught *Middlemarch* instead.

If only I hadn't found out I could have imagined her white with white.

But then if I hadn't found out it would never have occurred to me to imagine it.

Perhaps she is usually white with white – has been

white with white every other day of her professional life. (Or black with black – I'm not narrow-minded about this.) Perhaps there just happened to have been some entirely untypical disaster with the washing-machine, say, or some confusion in her packing for the trip, which would never be repeated, so that marking 'peach with white' against her name is entirely misleading. And since it will go on a file in the recesses of my own mind, a file to which other researchers can have no access and against which she can have no appeal, I have committed an injustice as pernicious as one of those secret security assessments which dog and destroy people's careers.

What am I supposed to do? Check it again? And then again? And then again and again and again? Allow her access to her file?

Omne animal post coitum etc etc. But was any animal ever beset by such a sheer range of post-coital concern as I am? From metaphysical horror at the flouting of a hitherto undiscovered divine sanction at one end of the scale, to the finest scruples at the other about the faint possibility of some injustice stemming in the remote future from my unfortunate discovery of a discrepancy in her underwear.

Not that its effects upon me were unfortunate. I was deeply shocked by this appalling solecism, it's true. But then I was moved by the artlessness of it. Suddenly she seemed hopelessly vulnerable, and of course at once I became wild to storm these melting walls. So then I triumphed in my pleasure and conquest; and she I may say in hers; and each of us in each other's. And part of my triumph was one sweet evil thought which I will confess to you, *hypocrite professeur, mon semblable et mon frère*, but to no one else. I couldn't help thinking that this was a revenge for all these long years when she had been up there, oblivious of me, and I had been down here gazing so intently up at her. Because here she was gazing no less intently up at me; and for that short time she knew me. She knew me as I knew her, and we were equal.

And this sweet evil thought was followed by another. In one huge bound, it occurred to me, I had overtaken the dreaded Impaler. He hadn't got this far in his researches. He was going to rush into print only half-prepared! While the wretched Dr Sproff, or Snoff, it seemed to me, would have been well advised to find some other line of work for which nature had equipped her better.

There. You've dragged it out of me at last. The whole truth, as always.

And so, with the sea breaking on the rocks, and the orchestra thundering, and the eerie horrors howling, and the little white scruples scrupling thinly in the wind, I will bring this mighty missive to a close. It is the day after these strange events, and the darkness is coming down again. I shall just have time to drop the letter in that post-box on the corner of Dirac Drive before I compose an expression of studious blandness on my face to baffle the envious and perhaps lubricious speculations of my colleagues at dinner.

Or rather before I *don't* drop it into the post-box.

Because I'm *not* sending it, am I. Quite apart from anything else, I don't know whether on an academic salary I can afford to post such a cargo of richly freighted prose to Australia at fifteen pence per extra ten grams.

But if I don't then it won't be curated where it belongs, with all the other letters in that ant-proof steel filing-cabinet of yours.

I shall leave the decision until I am standing in front of the post-box, and see which way my arm moves.

I WAS IMMENSELY IRRITATED BY YOUR LETTER. Entirely the wrong tone. This is because you wrote it before you received my last letter, which I wrote *after* meeting J L. By the time you read *this* letter, presumably, you'll have got the last one, and you'll have realized what a solecism you have committed. You'll have seen for yourself that we are no longer in the realms of *social comedy*. We are shaken by the winds of heaven. I have reached a *major crisis* in my life, and I have no one but you to turn to for comfort and advice. Facetiousness and flippancy are behind us. They belong to a youth which has suddenly expired.

I'm sorry. It's not your fault. It's the paleolithic slowness of aircraft between England and Australia.

The fearful truth is that I am in love. Possibly. Or possibly not. I am in *something*. Some state of distraction, anguish, irritation, regret, daydreaming, longing. I can't stop thinking about her. Well, obviously not – I've had classes to give on *TBAD*, and essays on her to set, and a paper on her to write for some drivelling publication in Arkansas. I've had to listen to la Foucault and others talking about her. I'm going to have to read twenty or thirty answers in examination scripts which misconstrue the plots of her novels and regurgitate some half-digested version of my own views on her – views which I see now were crass and immature, at once too high-handed and too respectful. How could I possibly stop thinking about her when she's my life's work? When I've only just met her and then lost her again before I could say any of the things I wanted to say, ask any of the questions I have spent the last twelve years waiting to ask?

Because lost her I have. I sent her flowers the very next day – did I tell you in my letter? Oh, you haven't got it yet. No, by now you have, we decided. What's happening to me? I can't remember anything (except her) from one moment to the next – I'm losing track of time – all the logical pins are falling out. Yes, I sent her flowers – £25 worth, not including the charge for phoning them, which is a lot of flowers. They should have got there before she did. By the time she arrived home the front doorstep should have looked like an altar. No name on the bouquet, no message – just this huge, wordlessly eloquent gesture. Or so I thought. Perhaps I should have put a name on them. Perhaps she simply couldn't guess who they were from. Because there was no reply. Not that I was expecting one, not that I was even hoping for one. All the same, I couldn't help noting that there *wasn't* one. Nothing. I also wrote a letter. Of course –

one always writes to thank visiting lecturers. So I wrote to thank, but in the most intimate and personal way. Then I rewrote the letter without the intimate and personal touches. Then I rewrote it again with a few sly allusions and innuendos. Then I cut out the allusions and innuendos. Then I tore it up altogether.

I was reduced to ringing. Got the answering machine. Her voice – but insultingly impersonal, shamingly stilted. She was not able to take my call just then, said this dreadful voice. Would I please leave a message. How could I leave a message? What message? I didn't know what I wanted to say! I was counting on some inspiration coming to me when I found myself in her presence – some new, suddenly remembered whisky bottle on the dressing-table. Your unconscious won't speak after the bleep! I rang again. And again. I rang late; I rang early. She was not able to take my call just then. Or just then, or just then, or just then.

I knew what she was doing. She was working. 'Do you work every day, or only when you're in the mood?' some idiot in my class had asked her – Jug-eared Jonathan from Jersey, *that* idiot – and she'd said something about always being able to work, no matter what. So that's what she was doing, quietly working while I failed to work. She was calmly scratching away with the Waterman, as if nothing had happened, as if I didn't exist. I was thinking about her, talking about her, hearing about her, and she was writing about someone else altogether. Some mere fiction. Some imaginary man who had some faint resemblance to a man she'd known twenty years before. Or no resemblance to anyone at all. And this faint, bloodless creature had pushed me out of her mind altogether.

But could she be working at ten o'clock at night as well as ten o'clock in the morning? Some other bean-brain in the class (Hazy Daisy, of course) had asked her whether she was a morning person or a night person, and I thought it was such a fatuous question that I hadn't bothered to listen to the answer. The opportunities I wasted! What did I think I was doing that day? I met her at the station off the 1809, arriving eight minutes late, which is 1817, and I left her in the guest-room at 0623. That's twelve hours six minutes, and at least seven hours of that I had wasted either sleeping or listening to other people make banal conversation to her – and apparently not even listening to the answers.

Hold on, you say. You have some faint notion that you have found a clue to the mystery. You suddenly see yourself as one of those tedious, bumbling characters in an old-fashioned detective story who turns out at the end to have solved the problem. Left her in the guest room, you query with deceptive mildness, at 0623?

Yes! What's odd about that? She was asleep. I didn't want to wake her up. All right? I needed to get back, have a shower, be ready for my first class. When was my first class? Not until eleven. As it happened. But I had to change my clothes, do this and that. Do what and what? Well, just possibly get an hour's sleep. Then perhaps get another hour's sleep. That's why I was awake at six. Because it was a single bed and I'd been lying on the edge of it. All night. She'd been in the middle of it, fast asleep, and somewhere around five o'clock, as I balanced, wide awake, along the six-inch ledge that remained along the righthand side, with my knees and arms projecting over the abyss, I began to feel an enormous resentment. It seemed to me that there was a mocking parallel between our positions on the bed and our positions in life. There she was, comfortably ensconced in the soft centre of English letters, not even aware that there were others clinging painfully to their outer edges.

I see some slight surprise on your face. Didn't I say I was in love with this woman? you ask. No, I didn't say I was in love with her, as a matter of fact. This is less than scholarly of you. Go back to the text. What I said was that I didn't *know* whether I was in love with her. I was in something with her, I declared. But what that something was had yet to be established. Possibly just a temper. Anyway, resentment wasn't the only thing I was feeling on the edge of that bed. I was also feeling tenderness and awe and a tremendous awareness of the soft pressure of her body all the way down my back. Also I was thinking about breakfast.

– What sort of breakfast? you ask idly. Orange juice? Eggs and bacon?

I don't mean like that. Well, poached eggs, perhaps, a little. Poached eggs and coffee. I had expended a fair amount of energy, after all. But the aspect of breakfast I was thinking mostly about was the sight of my colleagues' faces. I mean, as they raised their eyes from the *Sun* and *Private Eye* and saw me walking in. With her. All right, all right, not a very gallant anxiety, I see that – but I had to live with these people. To have broken a divine prohibition so solemn that no one had even known it existed was shattering enough, but for the entire Senior Common Room to *know* that I had would place an even more terrible burden upon me. I tried to think of it the other way round. What would *I* think if I looked up from my poached eggs one morning and saw – I don't know, I can't think of any parallels – Gavin Lecky in Animal Husbandry walking in with one of his pigs . . . No, no, no. Scrub that. But just think about this: I'm coming up for renewal this autumn. And don't say But everyone saw you buying those Durex Fetherlite. That was all rubbish. No one saw me buying any Durex Fetherlite, because I didn't buy any. They don't *have* Durex Fetherlite in the machine in the Students Union. (I've been saving up that crushing little rejoinder up for a rainy day, and a rainy day it now is.)

– Be that as it may, you walked out and left her breakfastless?

Certainly not. I wrote out the most precise instructions how to find the breakfast room, and left them on the bedside table.

– You amaze me. You are obviously much better organized now than you were in the old days. You actually had paper with you to write on?

In fact not. But that didn't stop me improvising.

– What did you improvise with?

The back of a cheque. Yes, yes – I can see that a cheque is not the most tactful thing to leave by a lady's

bedside in the morning. But it was either that or nothing.
Either that or no breakfast. Anyway, I scribbled out the
print on the front. Technically it wasn't a cheque any
more.

– Did you write 'Cancelled' across it?

Certainly not. Well, yes, I think I did. To be on the
safe side. In case it fell into the wrong hands. Look, it's
very easy for you to criticize, after the event, sitting
down there in the safety of the Southern Hemisphere. If
you had seen what I wrote on the back of that former
cheque I don't think you would have found it lacking in
tact or feeling. I not only drew a map showing the way to
the breakfast room, I even told her which urn the hot
milk was in and how to work the toaster. I said I'd
collect her in time to escort her to the station for the 9.37
back to London. And before you ask – no, I didn't
collect her. Because when I got back to my room I lay
down for the brief sleep I needed so as to ready myself
for the day's labours, and didn't wake up until ten to
eleven. When I reached the guest room after my class I
was not all that surprised to find that she'd gone. I didn't
attach too much importance to this at the time – I may
even have been, in the dark depths of my heart, a little
relieved. I sent off the flowers. (£25 worth, did I say?
Not including the cost of phoning them.) Then I went
singing to work, wrote that long letter to you (with a
lingering flippancy which I regret more and more from
one moment to the next) and that night went merrily to
bed. I laid me down in the middle of my own familiar
bed, as snug as a king in his kingdom, and dropped off as

sweetly as an egg off a table. Then, somewhere around two o'clock, I woke up – and everything was gone. All the merriment, all the snugness and sweetness. My peace of mind. My career. Possibly my sanity. This was when I got up to write the first version of the thank-you letter.

What am I going to do? I can't go chasing off to London. I can't just turn up on her doorstep. For her it was plainly a mere passing adventure, and it's over. I see that. I accept that. I'm nobody, after all. No, actually I'm not nobody! If we're talking about achievement, if we're talking about distinction, then you know and I know that it's a damn sight harder these days to get a job in a university English department than it is to get a novel published. I'm the one they should be asking for autographs, I'm the one they should be giving the lectures about! I mean, in cold sober fact, as we both know, that's the way round it is. Not that I'm laying claim to any superior status. To hell with the figures for books published and lectureships offered. All I'm claiming is that I'm me to me just as she's me to her, and me = me. I'm the sovereign of *my* universe just as much as she's the sovereign of hers, and I demand the normal protocol and courtesies that one head of state extends to another! That's reasonable enough, isn't it? I'm not saying something completely mad? What I can't bear is that for one moment she recognized my claims, acknowledged my rights. What makes me want to hammer my fist on the table . . .

Phone. Ringing. Hold on.

No. Just some student having a breakdown. Yes, what

makes me want to howl at the moon is the thought of her scratching away down there in London as if *nothing had happened*. I'd just like to know that she had lifted her head from her imaginary world for one moment, and said . . .

Another thought has just occurred to me, though. She may not be scratching away as if nothing had happened. She may be putting down some version of the events in the guest room. One of her maddeningly percipient, odd, crabwise heroines may be scuttering bizarrely sideways at the sight of some bumptious young academic's aubergine underpants. No need for one of your looks, thank you – I have managed to grasp the irony of this unprompted. It's different, though – she's not writing privately to a friend of hers in some comfortingly remote country. She's writing to friends of *mine*. And enemies of mine. And colleagues of mine. And students of mine . . .

What? *Are* my underpants aubergine? Of course they're not aubergine! Don't you know anything about my taste at all? But she may be *saying* they're aubergine! That's what they do, these people. They embroider, they improve on the truth – they tell lies.

Not at all aubergine, my pants, not faintly aubergine. Nor tartan, for that matter, nor spotted, nor leopard-skin, nor Union Jack. Nor peach. That particular pair, in fact, were pale blue. And that only because they got mixed up with something in the wash.

I'm sorry. I'm over-reacting. I know perfectly well that it takes years for events to percolate down into these people's unconscious. That in the process the identifying details get transformed beyond all recognition. That in any case *her* characters don't have comical adventures of the sort that she herself evidently has, and that if and when the episode ever does surface it will have been transmuted into some weird anguish involving flames and clairvoyant nightjars – will have become yet another station of the cross on some brave barmy woman's calvary.

I ought to be humbly grateful to be made use of. This is a privilege granted to few of us commentators.

Also, I ought not to have reacted in the way that I did to the prospect of the mismatched underwear. I see now that this reflects more on me than on her. You may think you detect, when the letter arrives and you come to read the passage concerned, a certain transferred sexual hysteria. If I could go back and correct the text, as you can and no doubt have been doing for the past seven years with your book on Mörike, I should remove all reference to it. Please bear in mind the unscholarly and exposed position I am putting myself in by sending off each episode of this story as it occurs, before its lessons have been learnt and its proper place in the whole assessed.

I can see already, for instance, even before this instalment leaves my hands, that I ought to have stayed and escorted her into breakfast. You were right. I was wrong. I think all my circumspection was wasted, in any case. The Pope was gazing speculatively at me over dinner that evening. I can read those looks of his as easily as the messages on hoardings. Perhaps he had been out there in the darkness on some jovial early-morning jog when I emerged from the guest room. Perhaps his television set had broken down, and he had nothing else to exercise his imagination upon. One way or another he had put two and two together, and made I should say at least 3.97. But then even my little Anglo-Saxon chum has got something into her head. I keep finding her wherever I go, bobbing awkwardly about in the shadows like an old tin can at the edge of the river. She makes funny little apologetic mewing noises, though what she's apologizing for I'm not sure. Being there, I suppose. Existing.

Oh, what's going to become of me in this life? I've been washed up on the beach and forgotten about. Nothing's happening in the world! Or if it is it's happening somewhere else. In Melbourne, perhaps. In London. Certainly not here. I see it now – I'm going to spend the rest of my life in this dreadful place. I'm going to die here.

I'm not going chasing up to London, though. I'll just lay my poor sad head down on my desk and . . .

I broke off there because I heard the postman.

And on the mat, when I got there, was a piece of thin cardboard, approximately fifteen centimetres by ten.

On the front: *Portrait of a Man Holding his Gloves*, by Jan Gossaert, 1470–1533, Busch-Reisinger Museum.

On the back the autograph inscription: 'Beautiful flowers! How sweet of you. J L.'

I am coming round to the view, as I study this document, that Jan Gossaert, 1470–1533, may be the greatest painter since Giotto.

And I ask you – can that woman write, or can she write?

There's a train at 2.57.

I HATE LONDON.

I hate all that wealth. I hate the way the money keeps leaking out of the rich bits and seeping into the poor bits like some oozing, radio-active effluent, and poisoning them. I hate not knowing where the contagion's got to now.

I hate people realizing I'm just there for the day. I hate other people who are just there for the day. I hate not being sure whether they are or whether they aren't.

I hate all those streets that somebody else owned on the Monopoly board. I hate those smug red buses that drop Monopoly names all over the front.

I hate the Dickens bits. I hate the Virginia Woolf bits.

I hate the weather. All that smart metropolitan hotness. All that savage metropolitan wetness. It was the wetness that got me this time. Blue skies and great rolling white clouds as the train came in through the suburbs, so I checked my umbrella in with my overnight bag in Left Luggage. I obviously couldn't arrive on her doorstep with the bag, as if I'd come to stay. I had to be just looking in, on my way from somewhere in London to somewhere else. And I obviously didn't want to arrive with an umbrella on my arm, looking like some cautious provincial academic who'd been forced to equip himself for all the day's possibilities hours earlier in some entirely different weather zone, when everyone in London knew there was some up-to-the-minute metropolitan dryness in the air. But when I came out of the Tube that bitch of a city had undergone some amusingly sophisticated change of heart. The sky was bleak, and an ominous wind was groping around inside my jacket and feeling up my trouser-leg. And, sure enough, by the time I had gone far enough to get lost it had started to rain.

It was one of those bits of London where with any luck you could get mugged by Rastas and vomited over by security brokers within the same block. Poor people desperate to be rich were all mixed up with rich people desperate to be poor, and the strangest anomaly on the streets was undoubtedly an academic desperate to remain an academic. Particularly an academic without an umbrella. The rain lost all normal civilized restraint. It hurled itself down on me with a terrible, impersonal metropolitan violence. My nerve broke. I ran. So that by the time I had found the right front door I was not only soaked but out of breath.

She took some moments to recognize me. She stood holding the door open with one hand, and holding a mug in the other with a plate balanced on top of it, caught between floors, probably, on her way from somewhere to somewhere else. She gazed at me, waiting for me to explain myself. I stood gazing back at her, not explaining myself. Why not? you ask. Because it took me some moments to recognize *her*. The last time I had seen her fully dressed – the *only* time – she had been wearing – I don't know – something kind of dark blue (you know how sensitive I am to colours). Something rather soft, with a touch of worldliness at her throat. I also recalled a waist, and ankles, and neatness in the feet. This is why I had been taken aback for a moment, as I had got to know her better, to find signs of such charming disarray beneath the surface. But now I was face to face with something in brown. A brown cardigan done up over a maroon dress over a pair of men's grey trousers over a pair of furry red slippers that some aunt had given her for Christmas. No worldliness, no neatness. No waist, for that matter, no ankles. Just a pair of joke halfmoon spectacles sliding down her nose. And a mug of tea, with a plate on top of it, and on the plate a slice of bread and Marmite with a tomato next to it.

I hated that tomato. It looked to me like a London tomato.

I say it took me some moments to recognize her. That's not so. I knew it was her all right – knew at once from that deep unblinking gaze above the glasses. I was just taken aback for a moment (once again!) to find it located in this dreadful bundle of old cast-offs.

Or, to be absolutely precise, I *should* have known at once it was her if I hadn't removed my own spectacles to wipe the rain off them. I put them back. And knew her. By which time she knew me. We knew each other.

'I was in town,' I said.

'Yes,' she replied.

We stood facing each other, waiting for something to happen. A difficult moment at the best of times, in my experience, the second meeting. But this was a tougher test than most. The wet trousers clung piteously around my knees like tearful supplicants. The terrible tomato rolled portentously around her plate like an oversized roulette ball that has still not made up its mind which of the players to favour. I knew what had happened. She had been working in some upstairs room. She had come downstairs to the kitchen for five minutes to get herself something to eat as she worked, and then before she could get back up the stairs – Porlock.

'Well,' she said.

'Anyway,' I replied.

I believe I told you in an earlier letter how much we had to say to each other. But we could get on equally well, I now discovered, without words. In fact after this opening conversation we were happy to stand for an hour or two in absolute silence. Then she moved to one side and gestured silently with the mug of tea for me to enter. The gesture dislodged the tomato, and it fell off the plate and rolled away across the hall. Even before I was properly through the door I was making haste to help about the house, as a guest should, by bending to retrieve it. She, like a good hostess, rushed to forestall me, so that I caught the mug and balanced plate with my shoulder. The tea went mostly over the wallpaper. The bread-and-Marmite fell on to the floor. Marmite-side down, of course. I hadn't just stopped her working. I had even stopped her eating and drinking. On the other hand, what a wealth of material I was giving her if ever, many years from now, when all this emotion is recollected in tranquillity, she attempts a comic novel.

Of course, as I stood in her kitchen drinking another mugful of the tea, I kept saying I was going to leave, but I felt it would be somehow improper to go wearing nothing but a flowered pink dressing-gown, as I was by then (my sensitivity to colour yet again!). I kept urging her to go back to work, but she could scarcely leave me in charge of a strange drier, with my shirt rumbling round inside it, or until the iron had warmed up sufficiently for her to iron my jacket and trousers. I didn't stand there in her dressing-gown doing nothing at all, of course. I wrung out a cloth and went back upstairs to the entrance hall while she called after me, 'What are you doing? Leave it, leave it!' and I wiped the Marmite off the floor and on to the wallpaper. I opened all the kitchen cupboards hopelessly, looking for more bread and more Marmite, and something to cut the bread on, and something to spread the Marmite with, while she cried, 'Leave it! *Please* leave it!' What else could I do? I couldn't go upstairs and write her book for her. Like a man on the high diving board I had moved to the edge by a series of acts which I myself had chosen and initiated. I had invited her to talk, walked her back to the guest room, hallucinated the whisky . . . But at some point I was no longer walking, no longer leaning out over space, no longer flexing and straightening the knees. I

47

was diving. The prerogative of choice had passed from me. I had become the helpless passenger of events. All I could do was hold the pink dressing-gown across myself with one hand, and with the other hopelessly open cupboards full of dusters and paintpots, and crumble the remains of the loaf under a blunt vegetable-knife. I had become a displaced person, shunted from one transit event to the next.

By this time, in any case, these events had got caught up and swept away in the general downtumble of events at large. She had to break off ironing my trousers to answer the phone, and the upshot of the phone-call was that she had to search the house for the *Collected Works* of Christina Rossetti, and her failure to find them meant that she had to make another phone-call to someone she thought she might have lent them to, and the troubles of the person she thought she might have lent them to kept her (and me) pinned in the kitchen until it was invaded by a huge confusion of very tall, lethargic young men, who all had names like Emmett and Tawney, and who turned out to be her two sons. I had seen the formula 2s. in her entry in the reference books, of course, and never taken very much notice of it. In small print, in the preliminaries to a long paragraph of titles and prizes and honorary doctorates, '2s.' is a neat little formulation, shorter and more transparent than H_2O. But just as out in the world H_2O can wash mountains away and soak suits and halt literary work, so in a small kitchen 2s. bulk much larger than honorary doctorates or membership of professional bodies. Very soon the room was completely full of them, draped hugely over counters, sprawling in chairs, eating, belching, complaining, fighting, asking for things, holding up the work on my trousers and rather conspicuously ignoring me, except to keep on requiring access to whichever small corner I happened to have taken refuge in.

Then things got worse. The room was suddenly, mysteriously even fuller. Perched on the edge of the table was a rather sordid man. I mean, *really* rather sordid, with grey hair, and a bit of a belly, and some kind of dreadful suede jacket. But I mean *curly* grey hair, and a shirt open down to here, and white socks, and battered soft shoes with little meaningless gold chains on them. Talking to her and looking at me at the same time, and swinging this terrible white-socked leg back and forth. Just suddenly *there*, on the edge of the table, swinging his leg, with no explanation of how he'd got there and no one taking any notice now he was. Talking to her, as she ironed my trousers, about various sums of money, and looking smilingly at me in my pink dressing-gown. And called something frightful like Bill, or Ben, when she got round to explaining me to him (she didn't explain *him* to *me*). And straight from some Book Fair, with his inside pocket full of twenty-pound notes. A second-hand bookdealer, in fact. Which is of course what Mr M, her former husband, had been. Funny, isn't it. And sordid. Furry slippers, and a dress over her trousers – and underneath this decent high-minded exterior a gross taste for men with a stack of used banknotes in their pocket and their feet in white socks.

I would have left as soon as I'd got my dry clothes back if it hadn't been for this gentleman's arrival. But as I padded upstairs with the clothes over my arm, and looked into rooms, trying to find somewhere to change, a bloody-minded mood came over me (and you know how bloody-minded I can be). It was something about the way he'd swung his dreadful leg back and forth and looked at me speculatively. Plus the rain, no doubt, and the Marmite. I was going to get dressed in the bathroom, but then I thought something like 'To hell with it!' and went into her bedroom instead. As I did up the buttons on my shirt I looked under the bed for shoes with functionless gold chains on them, and in the linen basket for soiled white socks (imagine the yellow stains on the sole!). Not a sign of him. He had access to the house without knocking, but he took his spare shoes and his filthy linen to some other establishment. Or establishments plural. Yes, quite possibly. That was the kind of man he was. I also looked through the crowded bookshelves that lined the room, and found a copy of that grim Canadian thing I contributed to, with copious reference to *TBAD*. It was under a pile of unsorted new books, and when I rescued it and opened it the compliments slip from the publishers fell out; it had plainly never been opened before. Another funny thing, when you think about it. I read every word she writes, even though not a single one of them is about me. She reads not a single word I write, even though most of them are about her. Well, to hell with it.

But it was ridiculous of me to notice such things, I

could see that. There I was, at large in her house, ideally placed to annotate and assess her habitat, and the only thing I'd managed to observe was my own article. So I made a conscious effort, as I sat at her dressing-table drying my hair with her hair-drier and combing it with her comb, to examine the reflection of the room behind my head. It was a great improvement on the university guest room. In fact I felt rather more at home there than I did in my own bedroom. The books around the walls absorbed all the sounds, so that one seemed to be thinking more quietly. Tiny possessions swam like brilliant tropical fish in little warm pools of light. The bed was modestly double. Yes, I think I can safely record in my notes that it was *a nice room*. So when I went downstairs, and discovered the 2s. gone, and the used-book salesman sitting at the table, with his shameful socks concealed beneath it, and a glass of wine in front of him, I sat down at the table too. 'I'm damned if I'll go!' I thought. I was greatly strengthened by being back inside my trousers, of course. I felt like Samson after a visit to a good trichologist.

J L poured me a glass of wine as well, after a slight but wounding pause, then left us sitting there while she cleared up the devastation left by the army of sons. Used Books smiled at his glass, and waited for me to leave. I scowled at mine, and waited for him to leave. 'So,' he said, 'what's going on in the world of Eng Lit?' 'Not a lot,' I whipped back. We sat and listened to the quiet, dull song of scourer on frying-pan. 'Well,' he said, 'I thought it suited you.' 'What?' I flung back. 'The dressing-gown,' he said. I was in no hurry to reply to this, but after a while I took a match out of the box that happened to be lying on the table and lit it. I watched it burn down to my fingertips. It took fifteen seconds, you will be interested to hear. I put the blackened corpse of the match down on the table. Then I took out another and did the same to that. Then a third, and a fourth. Some of them expired in thirteen or fourteen seconds. One of them I managed to keep going for sixteen. It was a large box, and the average contents, according to the label, were 300 matches. I believe I wanted to make it clear that I was prepared to sit there and burn each one down to the end. I believe I wanted to show him that I had unlimited time, and that I somehow knew that he had to get back to his wife, or to some other mistress, or mistresses. I could see out of the corner of my eye that he was watching the work on the matches, fascinated in spite of himself. I lit an eighth, and a ninth. J L wiped all the kitchen surfaces clean, dried her hands, and sat down at the table without pouring a glass of wine for herself. 'Is it a long journey back to wherever it is?' asked Dirty Books solicitously (one look at his feet and you knew his speciality was eighteenth-century erotica). I didn't reply. I laid out another dead match. I was arranging them in a neat line along the edge of the table. J L looked at me. I shrugged, and took another match out of the box. They both watched as I slowly, methodically burnt it to death. Books leaned his elbow on the table, and arranged his head on his hand so that he couldn't see me or my matches. He made a little conversation to J L about what

X had said Y's relations were to Z, where X, Y and Z were unknown quantities to me. But JL didn't respond; she was watching the slow cremation of her matches. As each match flared up it lit an answering spark in the depths of her eyes. After about the thirty-third match I realized her curly-haired friend had given up talking. He was watching as well. It was as irresistible as television. I began to feel like the producer of one of those series that everyone talks about in the Senior Common Room. London had a certain charm after all, I realized. After the forty-seventh match my opponent sighed and scratched his head. 'Well,' he said, and got to his feet.

Game.

As she saw him out I cleared away the burnt matches. I washed out the pornographer's glass, refilled it with wine, and put it on the table in front of the chair JL had been sitting in. Don't think I was making any assumptions, just because I'd outsat some greasy libertine in a suede jacket. Don't think I was remembering the modest doubleness of the double bed, and the welcoming intimacy of that little pool of light beneath the bedside lamp. It was the possibility of a divan in the living room that I was considering, that's all. It was going without breakfast, and shaving in the lavatory on the early train.

She came back into the kitchen and looked at her watch.

'I'm going back to work,' she said. 'Let yourself out, will you?'

And back to work she went.

I couldn't believe it. I thought I'd stopped her

working! I thought I'd destroyed her entire working day! What a waste of evil! All my boorishness – all my guilt – all the rich sense of irony I had felt at drying up the source of my own raw material – it had all gone for nothing! Which is why this letter comes to you on the back of someone else's typescript. No other paper with me – no more trains tonight – nothing else to do all evening in this dreadful little hotel with nylon sheets and no television. The only entertainment is sound. Channel One the sodden rain falling outside the window. Channel Two some stranded Indian (I assume) hawking and snorting in the next room. You think I like this city, I know that. You think I have some secret provincial ambition to live here. Well, I don't – I hate it. Or have I told you that already?

Writing on the back of things again! I suppose that's what my entire life consists in. If it's not cheques or discarded typescripts it's other people's books, other people's imaginations, other people's lives. Actually you may find the stuff on the other side of these particular pages more interesting than my hopeless adventures in Hell-on-Thames. It's part of a report on the running of Human Disciplines that we commissioned from some halfwit firm of management consultants. It's quite funny. Well, it made me laugh when I read it on the train. But that was yesterday.

That reminds me. How's yours? I mean your management consultant. Or wine-tasting consultant, or ear, nose and throat specialist, or whatever she was. (I'm away from my files, remember.) Mrs Thursday Afternoon.

Why do you always get mixed up with these strange wild gypsy creatures? Why don't you find yourself a nice steady woman, like me, who's too busy working to take any notice of you?

THANKS FOR YOUR LETTER. SORRY ABOUT THE weekend in Adelaide. And the cockatoo. Glad about your new lady-friend. Daniela, yes. The name alone would launch a ship or two. *Plus* lithe Thai thighs. Sounds like some new Oriental religion. And post-grad French Lit. – that'll make a change from water consultancy.

Sorry about your mother. Mine's on the blink, too. Knee, this time.

Nothing else happening here. Oh, Gordon has got Bradford. The chair. Gordon Wiley. I suppose you don't know him. Was at UEA after Norman. Bit of a tit.

What else? Computer's got the curse again. In fact the whole Department's having its monthlies.

The weather's rotten.

That's about it, I think.

Did I?

Sound depressed, I mean. Yes, well, I suppose I was. Can't remember, to tell you the truth. Forgotten when I wrote. It all just disappears as soon as it's happened. Don't you find?

Not even sure what I'm feeling now. Something. Something dull. Might be depression. Who knows?

Well. That's the way it goes. The weather, I expect. Also the usual business of where am I going, what am I doing? Etcetera etcetera. Etcetera etcetera etcetera.

Didn't I? (cf. para. 2 of your letter – 'mention Mrs M,' if you didn't take a carbon.) And yes, you're right. It does. (... 'mean things are not going too well on that front.')

Funny. You ask all these questions, but if I just gave you the answer, and didn't remind you what you were so concerned about, you wouldn't even know you'd *got* an answer. Forgotten questions and meaningless answers passing each other somewhere over the Indian Ocean at thirty thousand feet – an image of human communication. Of love and literature and life.

On second thoughts it doesn't. (Mean things are not going too well on that front, in case even the penultimate paragraph has already slipped away into the void.) It means that there never was a front. You can't have a front with only one side. *My* army was there, patrolling and shelling and suffering. But there was no army on the other side of the barbed wire. *They'd* left at breakfast-time after the first skirmish. I suppose it was that ridiculous sortie to London that finally made me see it. Well, I wrote to her a couple of times after that. I just wanted to open her eyes to her gentleman friend. I wasn't jealous. I haven't sunk far enough to be jealous of someone in stained white socks. I just wanted to tell her she was being used, treated as disposable property, like a second home, or a third car, or a fourth television. I just wanted to give her some proper idea of her own worth. But there was no answer. Not surprising, really, I suppose – I never sent the letters. Well, it was all a dream. A fiction. A private video inside my head to keep me going on the long ride from here to nowhere.

Read too many books, probably. Took the work too seriously. Conscientious little bugger, me. Always was. Natural swot. Think I'll cruise for a bit now. Plan my sabbatical.

Still got to teach *TBAD* in the interim, of course. So what? I can do it with my eyes shut.

I should have stopped at Henry James.

My mother's back in hospital. Other knee.

Amazing developments!

I hadn't rung the doorbell – hadn't even got to the front step – when the door's flung open and she comes running out, grabs me by the arm, and drags me inside. Speechlessly. Not a sound. No words of recognition – no explanation – nothing. Grab! In here! Me: 'Sorry, I just happened to be. . .' Be what? Never discovered. Because there inside is this extraordinary sound. It's like some kind of car-alarm – short bursts of enormous uncontrolled noise – but *animal*. It's coming from upstairs, and down the stairs, fleeing this terrible noise, is a *thing*, a huge and heavy something, falling crash, crash, crash from stair to stair, turning over and over as it comes, and throwing off bits like a Catherine wheel. It stops in the hall in front of me, and it's a *typewriter*, an upside-down IBM electric *typewriter*, trailing flex, and it lies as dead as a dead elephant in the middle of fallen hatstands and spread-eagled books and crunching glass and anguished sons. I run up the stairs, don't think twice, terrified, brave as a lion, towards this terrible sound. Some strange animal up there. Got out of the zoo. Can't see it because it's hidden behind a painful downpour of hard-edged black bouncing things, of black boxes, of black box-files, which hit my elbows and knees and spill huge swooshing slurries of paper guts. And there at the top of the stairs — the animal! No, animals, plural! Four, six, three of them! Animals in clothes, animals with arms and legs! Dozens of limbs and heads and trousers, all mixed up, all over the place — fighting – a battle. A man – no hair – berserk. A woman – fat – mouth open – blood on her face. Two people, fighting. Man and woman. Stop them, part them! Man shouting, woman screaming. Man assaulting woman – I've got it worked out at last. My God – rape! Stop *him*!

'Hold it! Fuck off! Fuck off!' Me to him this, probably. Trying to push him back. Trying to get hold of his flailing, raping arms.

'I'm the psychiatrist! I'm the fucking psychiatrist!' Him to me.

'Her! Her! Stop her! Get her!' From someone familiar on the stairs.

Scream – scream – scream. From the car-alarm with the open mouth, who's throwing muddled handfuls of manuscript into the air, kicking up childish little snow-flurries of manuscript – scroosh, scroosh. . .

STOP!

You to me, this. Because by this time, of course, you've got your breath back down there in Melbourne. You are being very calm, very reasonable. You simply wish to know what, *precisely*, is going on?

As if I knew! No time to explain, anyway. Agh! Someone's bitten my hand. Kick his bloody ankle! Get your fucking hands off me! Oh, it's you . . . What the hell are you . . .? My God! Boobla-boobla-boobla-boom . . .! That's two hundred LPs making their separate ways down the stairs . . .!

NO!

– you say, firmly but calmly. No, no, no. You want me to go right back to the beginning. Never mind what's coming down the stairs. You want me to explain how I came to be in her house in the first place.

– I've told you. She came running out . . . Sorry? You mean, how did I just happen to be standing there in the street at the time, given that the whole episode with her was over, that there never had been an episode?

Well, now. In the first place I wasn't standing in the street, I was walking along it. I was just going to ring her bell, on the off-chance, in passing, just as anyone might, if they found themselves in the locality of some old acquaintance . . . Yes! I genuinely was in the neighbourhood . . .! How? Because I had to go up to London for a rally. A *rally*. A union rally. Something political – you wouldn't understand. I know in the past I haven't always managed to do as much as I should to . . . Was the rally outside her house? No, of course it wasn't, but I had to go on from the rally to this other thing . . . That's right – I'd just reached her house but I still hadn't rung the doorbell. What's odd about that? You're not trying to imply that I was lurking about outside? Watching the house, or something? Too fearful to ring the bell? No, of course you're not . . . Exactly, it was pure chance. These things happen. They certainly do.

Where was I? Yes, *Götterdämmerung* and the Matthew Passion all over the stairs – and more people running up them, crunch crunch crunch. Red-haired woman with her hands raised imploringly. Two small children . . . A barking dog . . . Other people visible in doorways. Man with curly grey hair and suede jacket, *sitting*, hopelessly. It's all been going on forever.

You're holding your hand to your head again, I can see, very silently and patiently. You can't understand a word of this. No, well, I should think not. Nor can I – and I'm there in the middle of it all. I expect you'd like to be told for a start who all these people are. So should I, old cock, so should I! But one of the difficult things about battles, I can tell you, whether you're fighting them or whether you're describing them afterwards, is that people don't stop to introduce themselves. ('Hallo, there! I'm Colonel Bollockoff, 753rd Infantry Division. You must find all this awfully confusing, but what we're trying to do is to outflank you to the right, and then drop a small tactical nuclear weapon on top of you . . .') I'd never seen these people before! Well, the curly grey hair and suede jacket looked somehow familiar. Comfortingly familiar, I thought at the time, so I even misunderstood the bit I understood. I knew *her*, of course. Though I scarcely did, in fact, with her terror-stricken look in the middle of all this scream-shout-kick-pain-boombadoombla. I scarcely knew *myself*! I didn't seem like a self any more. I'd stopped being the general collecting-point for the universe, the organizing principle of creation. I wasn't at home to the world. I was out! I was just one more bit of the surrounding confusion. No, not even one more bit. Bits. Just a few more animal noises, a few more drops of flying blood and pumping adrenalin, another handful of unidentified arms and unexplained legs.

I can see you're looking very unmoved by all this down there in the placid State of Victoria, where the most violent thing that ever happens is probably the cans of peaches falling off the canned-peach trees. I'm not on the battlefield *now*, you object. I haven't still got my head wedged between the bannisters and someone's something while I'm writing this. I'm recollecting it in tranquillity, with the benefit of reflection. I'm reconstructing events. I must have done some historical research. I must have done *what*? What are you babbling about?

– There must have come a moment, you say patiently (I can see how you found out that wonderfully obscure fact about Mörike's childhood), when the jealous wife or mistress . . .

The who?

– The fat lady. There must have come a moment when she had subsided into tears and accusations and exhaustion, and been got out of the house by the husband, or lover, or led away by friends, or her sister, or sedated by the psychiatrist . . .

If he *was* a psychiatrist. He didn't sound much like a psychiatrist to me.

– . . . yes, and when the alarmed neighbours and next-door children had departed . . .

This was only after someone had called the police, you realize!

– Nevertheless, there must have come a moment when you sat down quietly . . .

Yes. On the stairs. I had to move the remains of the answering machine to find a space.

– Exactly. You sat down on the stairs, and presumably began to try to piece together what had happened.

Piece together what had happened? You mean, *ask* her?

–That's often the way people find things out.

How could I ask her? She was in a state of shock. She was walking up and down the hall, trying not to step on broken objects, and she was laughing shakily and crying, and she'd got her arm round one of her sons, and she kept saying 'Sorry' to him. And the other son kept picking up records and reading out the labels aloud and putting them down again. And then the telephone rang in the living room, and she just picked it up and listened and put it down again without saying anything. And you want me to start *interrogating* her? Well, I dare say Vlad the Mad would have got out his tape-recorder. Dr Scoff might have made a few notes. But I didn't even think of it. I was in a state of shock myself.

It's a funny business, I agree. Here I was at the very heart of the literary process. A uniquely well-qualified observer on hand at the beginning of creation. Because sooner or later she was going to have got all this arranged in her mind. Turned round backwards and shifted side-ways, with all the irrelevant participants, such as me, cut out of it, and all the others found names and faces and thoughts. There it would all be on paper. You'd know what everyone was doing and why they were doing it. You'd be able to hear what they were saying. You'd feel their pain and their humanity. And what would I emerge with, if I stuck to my trade? A page of incoherent jottings, which would be boiled down to make an awkward footnote in a memoir or a critical biography ('The author was present when events occurred which may possibly have suggested the scene under discussion here'), which would then be cut out at the request of her literary executors.

Still, that's the nature of the industry in which we work. I'm not complaining. I am acquiring certain insights, after all, even if they are incommunicable ones. Most people, probably, never see beyond the smiling, calm, confident public figure who came to be talked to by my students. What I saw today was a frightened helpless child, who had *gone too far*, and set the house on fire. I made her a cup of coffee . . . I'm lying – I made her a cup of *Ovaltine*, because that was what she wanted – and this time there were no impatient cries of 'Leave it!' as I hunted through the drawers and cupboards. She sat down in a little heap at the kitchen table with her head cradled in her hands, gazing down into the Ovaltine like an exhausted child. I watched her discreetly across the table. The smile had gone forever. That unblinking gaze was turned now not on the souls of men but on some dark vision in the depths of the Ovaltine. She was no longer extraordinary, no longer ordinary. She was an ingenious hard-working woman who had improvised some kind of rough shelter against the night winds and then seen it swept away.

The sons had left by this time – they had an important party to go to. (That's the difference between mere sons and someone who's teaching your books, you see.) I cleared a path up the stairs. I collected up all the manuscript. Couldn't help reading a sentence here and a sentence there as I did so, of course. It looked wonderful. There's a strange storm in it, when it rains gooseberries (cf. the second chapter of *Scatterbrain,* only there it's cornflakes), and something about a woman going mad on the Northern Line, which I found particularly sympathetic. Looked for the inevitable bonfire, beacon, flame-thrower, erupting volcano or whatever, but couldn't find it. No sign of any bespectacled young academic falling around at the heroine's feet, either. Not that I was expecting it, of course (not for another year or two, at least), but you can't help being apprehensive.

I laid all the manuscript out in front of her on the kitchen floor so that she could sort it. But she just shook her head. So I hoisted her to her feet, put my arm round her shoulder, and led her upstairs through the path I'd cleared. I didn't consult her; she didn't raise any objections; we said nothing. I put her down on the edge of her modest double bed. Unlaced her terrible old grey tennis shoes. Pulled her terrible old blue sweater over her head. Unbuttoned her terrible old faded trousers and stood her up while I pulled them down around her knees. Sat her down again and shook them off her, twisting her left

66

right left right left until they were free, while she sat gazing sombrely at her swaying knees. Then I lifted her feet on to the bed and tucked her up under the bedclothes, and all you can think of is what colour underwear was she wearing this time? Well, to hell with your prurient curiosity. I'm not telling you. To tell the truth I never even noticed. I wasn't looking at her like that. All I'm prepared to tell you is that she was wearing long navy-blue socks.

Still is, in fact. Because, although it felt as if the day had gone on for a lifetime, it was actually only seven o'clock. So I gently shut the bedroom door and finished clearing the house. Put all the books back on the shelf in alphabetical order. Checked all the records one by one. Lined up damaged machines by the front door ready to go to the repairer's. Hid all the irretrievably broken bits in black garbage bags. Found the vacuum-cleaner, but put it back and used brush and carpet-sweeper instead so as not to disturb her. Was an angel sent by God, in fact. Don't you wish you had some young pipsqueak studying *your* works?

Then I heated myself a couple of cannelloni in the microwave, and fetched a stack of her hundred-gram Conqueror bond out of her workroom. There being no other use I could think of putting my immense wakefulness to, I sat down at the kitchen table to write this dispatch. Now it's – my God – after midnight. I'm going to put my head round her door to make sure she's all right, then I'm going to settle down on the divan in the living room. Not since Boswell met Johnson has genius been so perfectly served. More of this anon.

More of this right now. Come running all the way
back to the kitchen to tell you. She's not asleep at all.
She's sitting up in bed with a stack of the old hundred-
gram and she's *working*.

VERY BRIEFLY, THEN.

(Sorry about handwriting. Living on this damned train at the moment – back, forth, back, forth – half meals eaten on it, most work done, in so far as work done at all just now – got class to prepare before we arrive today, in fact – but still can't write straight on table that keeps lurching about like drunken ouija board.)

You say in your letter that the events of Bloody Saturday may not have been as unconnected with me as I was letting you suppose. You suggest, in your most owlish way, that they may have been in some way ~~preeipa precipiti preeitipa~~ – oh this maddening train, why don't they try round wheels? – *set off* by my behaviour the first time I called. I don't see how, but then I wouldn't, would I, because I don't see anything. But yes, you may be right. Perhaps they were. Perhaps my arrival was just one card too many on the house of cards. I jogged the table – I breathed out at the wrong moment. *He* said something to some other him, some

other him spoke to some other her, some other her to yet
another her. . .

Not the pornographer's wife, you know, the human
car-alarm. Somebody else's wife altogether.

But yes, very probably. Who knows?

In fact, as I now see it with hindsight, the whole thing
– and it *is* a thing, I suppose I haven't told you, it's a big
thing, frighteningly big, the biggest ever for me, maybe
for her, who knows? and that's the second 'who knows?'
in as many paragraphs, which may suggest to you, and if
so, rightly, that the world has become a more mysterious
place to me in these last few weeks, a strange garden
where I walk with ~~aws~~ with ~~awo~~ – oh shit – with awe.
Just a moment – that sentence set out with some quite
other destination in mind – you see what a state I'm in.
Yes, this whole strange painful shimmering thing, as I
now see it, is in a sense my creation. I wrote the first
sentence, just as she might write the first sentence of a
novel. I invited her to come and be talked to, and from
that everything followed. Just as she might write at the
start of page one (indeed did write, at the beginning of
The Sunday Runners, though of course I'm quoting from
memory):

> The train stopped in a small grey town full of chapels and
> boarded-up warehouses. She could not see the name of the
> station. The only words visible were on small shops in the
> street outside. Fags 'n' mags, said one of them. Cash in a
> flash, said another. An old man in a ragged overcoat walked
> slowly down the street pushing a pram with a dog sitting in

it. No one got out of the train, no one got in. Discouraged, it began to move out of the station. The old man in the ragged overcoat stopped to wipe the drip from the end of his nose on his long woollen scarf. 'Here,' she thought suddenly. She dragged her suitcase down from the rack, opened the door and jumped down on to the slowly with-drawing platform. 'Here is where I will start my life.'

And from that one paragraph everything followed – the voices in the empty church, the death of the little Indian boy, the water-snakes, the dance in the perfume factory (and isn't that just the best single bit in any of the books? – just possibly in the whole of literature?).

Yes, I invited her. Out of nothing I made something. Out of the tangle of the world I plucked the one right string, and pulled, and lo, forth it all came, one strange event after another, like the water-snakes, like the knotted silk handkerchiefs from the conjuror's fist, crimson and sky-blue and orange and heliotrope. This whole great *thing* is my tribute to her – it's me doing what she does. Not in ink but in breath and in skin; not on hundred-gram Conqueror bond but on Wednesdays and Fridays and Sundays and Wednesdays and on all these desperate trains. She's the unknown station I jumped out at.

She writes the train; I ride it.

I did her one quite practical good turn, though. I think. My gradual reconstruction of the events at the top of the stairs leads me to believe that I may have saved a lot of her manuscript from being torn up. I remember now (or so it seems to me) that at one point in the struggle I was wedged up against a hand holding a frustrated, struggling slew of handwritten pages. I believe that it was only the enforced proximity of my left shoulder which stopped that hand joining forces with another vengeful hand somewhere on the other side of me to rip the pages into oblivion. What it was I saved, if I saved anything, I have no idea. But something, somewhere in her works, will owe its existence to me.

This may be the most important contribution I have ever made to my subject. Or ever will make.

I asked her about KG and DB, though. All these things are so easy when you're sitting at the kitchen table with a meal inside you and 2s. upstairs watching television, when you've at least half-an-hour in hand before you have to leave to catch the last train. If only I'd thought of this technique earlier in my academic career.

That's it, then. Twenty minutes left to prepare my Kipling class.

Did I ask after ~~Diane Davida~~ – oh, this bloody train! – your *copine* in French Lit. – Daniela?

Oh, she swore she'd never heard of her. Not Daniela. DB.

Have i ever told you what she's *LIKE*? i
haven't, have I! What am I thinking of?

She's like vanilla-flavoured cake. She's like a soft,
sharp cheese. She's like some kind of food you had when
you were a very small child that you get the taste of on
your tongue occasionally but that you can never identify
or locate.

No, she's not. She's like a new school textbook in a
dark-red cloth binding.

She's like one of those ordinary working days when
the air's fresh and the sun comes and goes; when everyone
in the streets is moving purposefully from place to place
in the middle of the morning, and so are you.

Do you think you can identify my assailant from that,
Inspector?

All right – perhaps I should simply give you a complete
physical description. I'll begin with her eyes, because
that's the first thing you notice about her. Her eyes are
like Indian groceries. That's to say, they're *open*. Very

73

open. Open from early in the morning until late at night. You have to watch them for a very long time to catch them blinking. I sometimes sit on the opposite side of the kitchen table and watch them for thirty or forty minutes without seeing it happen. A blink in her eyes is as rare as a sea-bream in the Sahara. Is it humanly possible to go that long without a blink? Perhaps she does blink – this astonishing thought is coming to me for the first time now as I write – and I don't see it because I'm blinking too. Her blink is unconsciously triggered by mine, or mine by hers, so that we blink in perfect unison.

They're serious eyes, that's the next thing you notice about them, and they shine in the soft light reflected upwards from the tabletop beneath the shaded table-lamp. The pupils stand wide in the half-darkness, and in each of them is a tiny man. This tiny man fits into the pupil most perfectly, like a jewel into a jewel-case. His appearance is striking. He reminds me of a small golden cloud left in a clear evening sky, or a smile left in the bathroom mirror. No description of her would be complete without a complete description of him, so I'll start with his eyes, since they always seem to be looking at me. They never blink, either. They're not so serious as hers, but they also shine in the soft upward light, and the pupils are wide. But what makes them immediately recognizable is that in each pupil is a little woman. Now, no description of the little man could ever be exhaustive unless it included a description of the little woman in his pupils . . .

I'm sorry about all this. It's probably because it's the

fourteenth of the month. Which, as psychiatrists now recognize, is three days after the eleventh.

She's forty-four, you know. Quite matronly. Wears spectacles to read. Doesn't laugh – never laughs.

I'm thirty-two. Thin as a sheet of paper. Have to keep my spectacles on until my face is about sixty centimetres from hers. Enjoy an occasional laugh.

Another bulletin very soon, then, with a full update on the situation as it develops. P L U S academic gossip, film reviews, cookery tips, polite inquiries after you and Daniela – and much, much more besides!

First, an apology. I realize I haven't written for, well, however many months it is. So long, anyway, that your end of the correspondence has finally guttered out as well. But I think you'll understand how very fully occupied my waking hours have been when I tell you that I'm getting married.

Tomorrow.

In fact, this letter is by way of being my stag night. I've eaten a good absorbent chicken and rice in the Faculty Dining Room to line my stomach, then come back to my room and set a large tumbler of straight malt on the desk beside me. May I ask you, before we go any further, to supply yourself with a similarly excessive amount of whatever you keep at the back of the cupboard for special occasions. I'll sip as I write, you'll sip as you read, and we'll both become a little lachrymose as we look back together upon the old glories, and forward to the uncertain splendours yet to come. We may even end up singing and smashing street-lamps. Or reading-lamps.

In fact my regular badminton partner here, a dim good soul in Business Administration, very kindly offered to round up a few colleagues and take us all into town for an evening of ritual debauch, with a taxi ordered for afterwards. I told him I had work to finish. One other stag, and him in Melbourne, is stag night enough for me. A quiet stag-to-stag is what I feel like. I realize that in the past I have not always revealed my deeper feelings. I'm changing, though. When you've had a moment to get over your initial shock at my announcement I shall talk to you rather seriously, in a way that you may find surprising, even embarrassing. But you won't be there to enjoy the public emotions of the ceremony tomorrow, so you'll just have to have a private preview of them tonight.

You will be most sorely missed tomorrow, incidentally. It's at her local registry office, with no one but us and her sons, plus her agent and sister as witnesses, and not a soul on the bridegroom's side of the nave except possibly my mother, *if* she can get up the steps. There's a small contingent from the Department (organized by the Beldam, of course, not me) travelling down to the reception afterwards, which we're giving in a restaurant we've heard good things about, especially from our old friend Ben, a rather crooked but amusing rare-book dealer, whose son runs it. Apart from them I shall be all alone.

Bridegroom. Reception. These are sonorous words. You're going to start wanting to know the composition of the bride's bouquet, and the colour of her going-away dress. These details are still secret, from me at any rate, but I can exclusively reveal where the happy couple will

be going for their honeymoon – straight back to the
bride's house, in the case of the bride, who has a rather
difficult chapter to finish, and straight back here for the
bridegroom, who has an examiners' meeting. It's going to
be a working honeymoon.

Bride. Yes. Another word that goes echoing away
down the corridors of the mind. *My* bride. A double
echo, like the key turning in some mighty lock. But this
is what she has become. Because make no mistake –
when I say bride I mean bride. And when I refer to her
as my wife, which is what I shall be doing the next time I
write to you, my wife is what I shall most solemnly
mean. So, as you can see, I have changed. I don't have to
tell you, of course, how seriously I have always taken her
work. How seriously I have always taken its *seriousness*.
This is what I admired in her from the first, and this is
what I have come to love. The noble tradition to which
we all once paid homage – the tradition of literature as a
moral force – is alive and well and living in my bride, my
wife-to-be. Not for a moment was she ever distracted from
it by the fashions of the day. It is present in every
mystery that she admits us to. Whereas I, even in my
letters to you, have leaned a little towards the deconstruc-
tionist at times. My weakness for the light ludic touch
may even have misled you about the strength of my
feelings. I have been a comic novel. I see that now. I do
hereby rewrite myself. I do most solemnly abjure my
lightness, and strike my jesting words from the history of
the world. I declare them unsaid.

I look back to the beginning of this letter and already

even that seems to belong to the past. I see to my astonishment that I said I was getting married. What a strange way of putting it. There are two of us involved in this business, after all. *We* are getting married.

Our first truly corporate act will be to move. I should have been perfectly happy to shift my last few pairs of clean socks into her present house and inscribe myself on the local electoral roll. But I can't go on commuting from London, and she can write anywhere, so we have bought a house about fifteen minutes' drive from the campus. (Or what will be fifteen minutes' drive once I've learnt to drive.) It's one of those leadenly suburban-looking houses you sometimes see dumped down in the middle of the countryside, as if they'd come on a day trip wearing unsuitable dormers, and then got lost and sat down to rest their rosebeds. But it's quite big, and by the time our builders have blocked up some of the frightful picture windows, put in a mile or two of bookshelf, and chipped out several acres of blush-pink bathroom tiling, we shall be ready to welcome you for literary weekends around the log-effect gas-fire.

And don't think I'm not aware that she's the one who is making the sacrifice. London doesn't mean very much to me, but it does to her. How's she going to manage without her little Indian grocer's, or the office-supply shop in the High Street where she gets her paper, or the woman in the cleaner's who tells her who's up to what with whom? What's she going to do without her friends and their muddled lives? And without her enemies? She needs enemies, you know. One does. We all do.

Why did she do it? Why did she say yes? Well, why, in the first place, did I ask her? No mystery about that. I wanted to ask. I had to ask her. I had to try it. I had to see whether she'd say yes. You can't stand still in life. Trees and rocks can stand still, but living creatures have to keep moving. Stand still and you've only the rocks and trees for company. You've got to go forwards. Don't you feel that? Forwards, forwards. I suppose that's why she said yes. Not much else in it for her that I can see.

I asked her in the Indian grocer's, incidentally. If you're interested in that sort of piquant detail. It was one of those muffled vague London Sunday mornings. She was standing in front of the refrigerator section, picking up tubs of cream and trying to read the dates on top, screwing up her eyes because she couldn't see without her glasses. I was carrying a wire basket with the papers and a loaf of bread and a box of eggs and a large pack of toilet rolls, and I opened my mouth to say something to her, I can't remember what – I think something slightly impatient about her slowness – and somehow the words changed in my mouth. It was the sad poor smell of the shop. I suddenly wanted to take her away from all those dubious pots of single and double cream, away from all these half-cock bodged-up indeterminate Sundays. Away from her tiresome London. 'I wonder if we should get married,' I said. She looked at me. I looked at the packs of streaky bacon. Then she went on examining the tubs of cream. I thought she hadn't taken it seriously. I wasn't hurt. I didn't necessarily require a response. The words had got themselves said; that was the essence of the thing. Then, after we'd come out of the shop, as we were walking back to her house, she said: 'I suppose the boys could live with their father for a bit.'

Why do they do it? Any of them? What do they see in us? Another glass? Why not. Don't have a stag night every night.

At least I shall be able to protect her privacy a little more closely in the country. She's at everyone's mercy in London. There's something about her writing that makes people want to invite her to meet them, or invite themselves to meet her. Complete strangers turn up on on her doorstep and expect admission. The other day some couple arrived from Nagasaki, in tracksuits and inscrutable smiles, with various works of hers they wanted signed – *thirty-seven* volumes, brought all the way from Nagasaki in an old Sony television box. If she's opened the door herself and come face to face with someone she can scarcely just slam it shut on them again, but any literary gawpers who struggle out to Windy Ways (as it's called, until we get round to changing it, in cursive across an untrimmed slice of tree-trunk, like a squiggle of Worcester sauce across an open sandwich) will be faced with me on the doorstep, if they are not sent reeling back to town first by the sheer embarrassingness of the name. I shall be as thorough as Mr Rochester in keeping her out of sight. I'll get to the mail first. All long rambling letters from people with personal problems and literary aspirations – straight into the recycling sack. All invitations to visit remote cities and dim universities – pulped unread! Another twig of another tree saved! My natural vileness will rescue her from her own good-heartedness.

And what deep reserves of vileness are indeed stirred by the sight and sound of one's fellow-enthusiasts! Their woozy gushing seems to parody and devalue one's own hard-won, measured appreciation. I shall take particular pleasure in seeing off all the other academic bloodsuckers. Any imperious cables from the dreaded Impaler, any fourteen-page questionnaires from the dyslexic Dr Shroff, and I shall write the replies. I think the Impaler had better start sticking his pins into wax images – Dr Sploff had better acquire some alternative qualifications in accountancy or book-keeping. Taking me, my bride is, and forsaking all others. Sorry. A faint suspicion of the ludic there. A last sip before the bottle's thrown into the bin. Speaking of which . . .

I give you . . . the bride and bridegroom! A slightly premature gift, but no one's going to be giving you us tomorrow. JL and RD. JL – that's still how I refer to her, still how I think of her. I wonder if should try abbreviating it to J when we're actually man and wife . . . What does it sound like? J . . . *J* . . . 'Listen, J . . . Is that you, J . . .? How do you feel about it, J, love . . .?' She calls me Richard, incidentally. I can feel myself blushing.

No. I'll stick with JL. That's a decision.

I've no thought, naturally, of turning my privileged position to my own academic advantage. Quite the contrary – I may have to give up teaching her. I'm not sure whether one can stand up in a lecture-hall and expound one's wife's thoughts, hazard guesses at one's wife's intentions, extol one's wife's moral seriousness. I may be professionally done for – may even have to get out the old Conrad notes instead, or start reading long novels by drunken Americans. I'll confess now that I once had genuine hopes of writing a study of her work myself. Another ambition gone. On second thoughts, though, why not? Why should I clip my tiny wings any further? There are precedents. There must be. Anyway, why do I need precedents? Everything in this world is different from everything else. Every person is the first and last of his line. Every relationship is the only one such. In fact, I recall a conversation with you, many years ago, on this very subject. You were talking about your relationship with some unsuitable girl, and I said something about relationships being like suspenders. No – *you* brought up the idea of suspenders, and I said . . . something true and wise, though what it was I've forgotten. In fact what all this has got to do with the matter in hand I have no idea. I seem to be getting somewhat confused.

We were sitting on the parapet of a bridge somewhere. It was late at night. We were both saying true and wise things. I suppose we were pissed.

So this is how the story ends. Not been without its peripetetia, this story of mine. Something funny about that word. Its peritapetia. No. Its twists and turns. Might be a few more still to come, if Ethelburga takes it into her to head to show up at the reception tomorrow. My little Anglo-Saxon. But that's another story. I don't flatter myself I was ever much in control of that one. I was just the proximate cause, the bump in the road that brought the whole rickety load tumbling off the back of the lorry. It was just an accident waiting to happen.

Whereas with this one . . . I wasn't in control exactly. I'm not claiming that. But I did give the first little push, didn't I? I didn't just lie there like a bump in the road and wait to be run over. I got up and waved my arms and made her swerve. Didn't I?

I don't know. Did we ever do anything, you and I? Or did it all just come tumbling down on top of us?

Do you know I once won the Sydney and Louisa Dibdin Prize for English Composition? Little did I think, as the assembled school applauded and the Chairman of the Local Education Committee pressed the richly inscribed book-token into my hand, that I should end up married to one of the major writers of our time.

Little did I think, for that matter, that I should end up married.

Little did I think, period.

No, bollocks. Not little did I think at all. Big did I think. I thought I'd end up married all right – married to the wife of one of the major writers of our time.

Here it is, then. My stag letter. Lying on its back with its legs waving in the air.

It was that one near the old cardboard-box factory. The bridge we sat on.

Got to get up in five hours' time. Do my stuff. Woo-hoo.

THANK YOU. IT'S A LOVELY THING TO HAVE, AND I'm deeply touched that you went to so much trouble.

Actually, this thank-you letter is so insanely late that you've probably no longer any idea what I'm thanking you for. It's for the present. You sent me a present, remember? A great brown-paper parcel. Air mail. Lots of stamps with koala bears and wallabies and things, only not enough of them – I had to pay £4.20 excess postage. I'm joking – of course there were enough stamps. Inside – a book. A rare first edition, of a work by some rare Australian writer. So rare that I can't tell you offhand who it was, because I put it carefully away on the new bookshelves, which we've now at last got arranged in proper alphabetical order, and I can't remember what letter his name started with.

No, it really did give me a great deal of pleasure. What's only just come back to me, though, is why you were giving me a present in the first place. It was a wedding present. Because – that's right – we got married!

My God, that was a long time ago – I'd forgotten I was ever single! What I think I'm trying to say, as you no doubt realize, is that *we* are touched, grateful, etc. After all these weeks – months even – of being married I'm still not quite used to the conjugal we, or the impersonal tone of the joint communiqué. It gave *us* a great deal of pleasure. Didn't it, dear? Yes, she says. What, darling . . .? Yes, my wife joins me in expressing our heartfelt thanks and appreciation. Actually she doesn't, because she's upstairs working. I made that bit up. Something to bear in mind, as a matter of fact, if you ever contemplate marriage to a major writer of our time. It's six o'clock on Sunday evening, an hour when most of the other couples in this rural paradise are well into the first bottle of Frascati (or so I should imagine from their appearance – we haven't attempted much social intercourse with the natives). And where is she? Away in the lands of Faerie, returning who knows when. This is life with a Maj-WOOT – it's largely life without a MajWOOT.

In fact, this place is ideal for her. I feared she might go into a decline without the reassuring presence of dreadlocks and drunken Irishmen. But she seems entirely happy with flowers and cows. She's out in the garden half the time, in fact, deadheading the greenfly and mulching the cucumber frame. And when she's not in the garden she's baking unsliced bread, and cycling over to the Village Stores (est. 1876) for bulk supplies of organic flour and wholemeal potash. Which is of course one of the reasons she's still upstairs writing at ten o'clock at night. Another reason being that she is working on a very long book, and yet another being that she would be anyway.

No, the one who's suffering is me. I have a job to go to, but no car to go to it in because the local examiners refuse to recognize my poststructuralist style of driving. I have had to buy a dreadful kind of two-wheeled Japanese sewing-machine, and another pair of L-plates. Since then I have had no head. I have been struggling to think with a large maroon-coloured metal football instead. For the first few weeks this football went around attached to a few attributes you might have recognized as mine – a pair of herring-bone tweed arms and a couple of smoke-grey corduroy legs. But there is a limit to the number of times you can take a class on George Eliot, or even George Gissing, with sodden smoke-grey corduroy around your private parts and the icy wind still trapped in the weave of your herring-bone. So now I have vanished completely. Some strange figure in sadomasochistic boots and maroon plastic packaging clomps in to take my classes, and wobbles home to make love to my wife. So detached do I feel from him, in fact, that I have let him go on teaching my wife's books. People gave him a few odd looks for a start, asked a few impertinent questions. But then they forgot about it, as they always do. He's perfectly objective about her – is a little cool, for instance, as I used to be, about the short stories. By the time he's got home and taken all his equipment off, in any case, he's in no condition to begin getting up long novels by some other twentieth-century woman writer as an alternative.

No, when I come back in the evening and hang my

head up on the hatstand I hang my troubles up with it. And make no mistake – I've done my bit about the house with the white emulsion and the Black and Decker. This is why I'm so behind with my correspondence; every spare moment has gone into adapting Windy Ways to her ways and my ways. We kept the name, in the end, because we couldn't find any alternative. Not for want of trying; I racked my helmet for weeks. All names ending in House were too large; all names ending in Cottage too small. We thought of literary names, like Erewhon and Nightmare Abbey, and I could feel the sweat running down inside my plastic leggings. I wanted to give it an arbitrary number, like 7057, but the council wouldn't accept it. I suggested Majwoot's, but the majwoot herself didn't understand the word. At this point I reached the end of my imagination. I am a little inhibited about names in general, I realize. I feel a little bashful about squirting myself over the world like a dog marking the lamp-posts. Whereas she, of course, is naming away in her books all the time. Names, names, names, and never a second thought. That's one of the differences between us.

So, 'Windy Ways' has the attraction of not having been chosen by me, and Windy Ways it is. Also it's so wonderfully awful that it's plainly not supposed to be taken seriously. And then again she actually likes it. Don't you, dear? She's smiling enigmatically. Or she would be if she were here. Since she's not I can tell you something rather remarkable that I have discovered about her these last few months: she has very simple tastes. In fact she is a very simple person. This is her secret.

So am I, now I come to think of it. At any rate I enjoy being a simple housewife while she's working. I've just slipped out between paragraphs and set the supper, for instance. Cold beef, a good winter salad and a loaf she baked, nicely laid out on a fresh white tablecloth. All she has to do is come down and eat it. This is how we share the chores. I do the jokes and the salad; she does the bread and the sincerity.

Eight o'clock. I've just taken a stroll out into the front garden. You can often see me out there at some point in the evening, standing on the stack of bricks which are waiting for the builders to come back (to make a wall for the peach espalier we are going to have) and gazing up at the roof. I'm looking at the dormer window on the right. There are no curtains yet, and you can see her shadow, cast by the light of the desk-lamp. It lies along the white slope of the ceiling behind her, sometimes so motionless that if you didn't know what it was you'd never guess it was the image of a living creature. Then she sits back in her chair, and the shadow abruptly swells, violently pregnant with sudden thought. But what the thought is remains as shadowy as the head that thinks it.

So what's it about this time, you ask. What's what about? Oh, the book. Hold on, I'll shout up the stairs . . . What's it about, sweetheart. . . ? No answer but a dog barking somewhere, and a distant car. No, in actual fact I don't ask. Why not? A certain delicacy of feeling. Or possibly because she might tell me. Don't I want to know? Of course. I long to know. I just don't want to be *told*, somehow. I want to find out for myself in the same way as I always did, by reading it.

Perhaps it's about the simple rhythms of the rural seasons. Perhaps it's a *gardening book*! Oh, my God, what have I done to her? No, I suppose she's got plenty of urban raw material stored away. Her life was quite complicated, you know, until I came along. Amazingly complicated, for such a simple person – I'm only finding out quite slowly what a tangled web she has woven over the years. Suddenly, over the washing-up, apropos of nothing, some astonishing revelation. I feel quite jealous. Of course, she's had twelve years longer than me to accumulate it all.

But now her life's as simple as she is. A few dramas with the slugs, a certain clash of ideologies with the people who did the wiring, the occasional 2s. at the weekend, doing their best to provoke a double murder. The Beldam has invited us to dinner, of course, and Pope John XXIV has blessed us over the claret. They make a poor contrast with the kind of people who used to borrow money off her in London, in their colourful metropolitan way, and have babies in her spare room, and cut their wrists in her kitchen, and otherwise enrich her life. But I think she could squeeze a satirical chapter or two out of the Beldam, or the Popess, if only she could learn to write satirically. I am offering her the possibility of growth up here.

She could always write about me, of course. Us. Our story. I can imagine how she would handle some of the episodes. There's something about the Battle on the Stairs, for instance, that reminds me of the Wild Children's Halloween party in *FDDS*. It could turn out to have the same kind of mythological resonance. I suppose I shouldn't come out of it all that well – a bit like K in the book, probably. Rather short on sensitivity and understanding. Still, he had a good heart. As I understand him, though the Spoff woman disagrees. She, in her wisdom, sees K (and would no doubt me too) as the archetype of masculine destructiveness.

So, there we are – the literary life at last. Work and work and bread and work. Oh dear, though. Looking back over this letter I see I've already slipped into a humorous husbandly tone of voice. I had a plan to become serious. In fact I am serious. About one thing in this world, at any rate, and that's her seriousness. Sharing the same toothpaste has not reduced the honour in which I hold that. And her.

I put that bit in quickly because here she is, walking amongst us, all hallowed by her labours, and ready to eat . . . She's coming over to the table . . . She's looking abstracted – she's going to eat me by mistake . . . No, it was a kiss. I'm sorry – this is getting very sugary. Time for you and me to go our windy ways.

Oh, bugger! I should have asked how Diane was!

No, I shouldn't. Because she's not called Diane. I've done it again. When my party comes to power we're going to abolish names. I shall think of her as D. How's D?

A VERY HURRIED NOTE TO SAY HOW TRULY SORRY I am about Daniela. Unforgiveable of me not to write before, after your first great bust-up with her in the car-park outside the French Department. But then you wrote to say it was all on again . . . I can't believe I didn't write *then*. Oh Christ. I can only say that I've been busier these past few months than I have ever been in my life before. Not with partings and reconciliations, like you – not even with departmental budgets and examiners' meetings. With aunts and uncles. Also mothers and great-nieces. The majwoot has picked up old buckets and boxes in the dark corners of my life and found all these creatures creeping about – cousins and mothers and people I scarcely knew existed. Did you know I had a second cousin who holds a very senior position in the West Midlands Regional Health Authority? Of course not – I've kept the old newspapers on top of his hiding-place, and if by some chance you'd picked them up and discovered him you'd have been polite enough to put them back again without inquiring further. Not so the maj. Who's this? How's *he* related to *her*? We've been crawling into little nooks and crannies all over England shaking their feelers. She puts down pots of home-made jam for them and gives them strange woolly garments to munch. So naturally they've been scurrying out into the light and infesting the spare room here. They think she's crazy. No, they don't, as a matter of fact. They think she's wonderful, just as everyone else does. We've seen my mother more often this summer than I remember seeing her when I was a boy. Up and down the motorway we've been ever since I passed the test. Wrecked the car, in fact – no one told me you had to put oil in it if you're going to go screaming all over the country looking at mothers. So now I'm back on the bloody Kawasaki. At least Daniela's spared you all that kind of thing. No, sorry, that's absolutely crass. All part of the terrible smugness of marriage. At least you're avoiding that. I do in fact realize how you must be feeling. I'm just a little distracted because I can see some of them in the garden. I mean some of these things out of the family woodwork. Funny – she slaughters the centipedes and replaces them with pests that are about a thousand times larger and five thousand times more destructive. Now of course she's upstairs working and they're bashing about around her esparto grass with a football, totally bored, and I know that sooner or later if I don't go out and entertain them they're going to . . . They have. Sorry – write a proper letter tomorrow.

CONGRATULATIONS NOTABLE UNION GERMAN and trench lit. Hope life together in double lit will yield much satisfaction. Last bit was for best man to read out at reception. Sincere delight amazement best wishes love us both you both. Extravagant present follows. Also letter.

Here you are, then. One wedding present, slightly foxed. Couldn't afford to airmail you a toaster, but we thought *Goethe* writing about a campaign against *France* had a certain witty relevance in the circumstances. No? Well, perhaps not. Use it as a doorstop, then. Not a first edition, I'm afraid, but Berlin 1863 sounds like an interesting little vintage. Proper letter shortly.

Wishing you a Merry Christmas and a Happy New Year!

She bought this bloody thing, not me. Waiting with some interest to see whether you've been reduced to Christmas cards as well. Oh, thank you for thank-you letter. Will write.

Venezia: Tramonto sulla Laguna.
Venice: Evening sunlight on the Lagoon.
Venise: Effets de soleil sur la Lagune.
Venedig: Sonnenuntergang auf der Lagune.

Not much room left to say anything else. But then not
much else left to say. Here to work. *I* am – conference on
the European Novel. Also to stop her working, and
adding to the problem for the rest of us. Nothing else to
do here, though – wettest April in Venice since 1647.
Effets de pluie is all we've seen on the *Lagune*. Love. Will
write.

Best Wishes for a Happy Christmas and a
Prosperous New Year.

My God – Christmas again! What's happening?

We're both well. How about you? Will write.

Which reminds me – I get occasional postcards and Christmas cards from someone in Melbourne with that signature – Will Write. Could be a relation. Don't know him, do you, by any chance?

CONGRATULATIONS ON CHARLES JAMES BREWETT Edward. The name alone is the longest communication we've had from you since you got married. I very much admire the way it starts quietly, like an old-fashioned novel, with several chapters of exposition, then suddenly bursts out into the entirely unexpected vehemence of 'Brewett', followed by the quietly happy ending of 'Edward'. Eight pounds three ounces — that sounds a very healthy weight. Is that just the name, or is that the baby as well?

Anyway, well done, all three of you. I now feel very guilty that I didn't send you a card to announce the happy event at our end — the arrival of *The Invisible Banquet*, a much-wanted little brother for *The Book of Angels' Dreams*, *The Sunday Runners*, *Falling down Duke Street*, *Scatterbrain*, *Whistling Woman*, etc. Ten pounds five ounces, our little monster — I've just weighed the typescript. The precious bundle was put into my arms six weeks before Charles James etc. saw the light of day, and I should be happy to share with you the experience I have gained of fatherhood. It's a difficult time for the father, don't you find? You don't have space on your printed card to go into all the details of pregnancy and labour. Did you go to classes yourself to prepare? Was it a natural birth? Were you present? Did your baby have to be sent away for typing? Ours was so natural that I didn't even realize it had happened. I'd forgotten the maj was pregnant, to tell you the truth, it had all gone on for so long. Or rather I'd forgotten pregnancy was a condition that ever came to an end. So when Her Maj came downstairs that evening – it was a Tuesday, just after seven o'clock – and said, 'I think that's very possibly it,' I didn't faint or burst into tears. (Did you? I do find the text of your card most perversely laconic.) I merely inquired '*What's* very possibly it? What's very possibly *what?*' Didn't I, dear? She's smiling at the memory. I may even have spoken with slight asperity. I thought she was referring to some private thought of hers about the garden – she was gazing absently out of the window at the time. It crossed my mind that she might just possibly be announcing the end of our marriage. Did I snarl, darling? I can see from her expression that I did. Probably there was no such ambiguity over the arrival of C J Brewett E.

Have you suffered from the traditional feelings of jealousy and exclusion since, though? I've felt twinges, I must confess; I think sometimes that I should have found some preparatory classes to go to, and got myself in the right frame of mind for fatherhood. And that's another question. *Am* I the father? I talk about 'our' book, and dandle it fondly on my knee. I even occasionally change a dirty spelling. But did I in fact have anything to do with it? There's some uncertainty as to the date of its conception. It's different for you. You know the date of D's last period – may even recall a particular night when the ovum was ripe and the moon was high. But who knows even in which month an idea is planted in someone's mind? I probably didn't tell you at the time, because it made such a misery of our first months together, but an earlier book miscarried. (So all that manuscript I saved for posterity in the Battle on the Stairs went the same way as yesterday's papers.) When she subsequently started *The Invisible Banquet*, was it ours – or was it from some dreadful old frozen sperm she'd found at the back of the refrigerator? That's what they do, you know, these people. Where you keep a few bottles of the local Coonawarra Riesling chilled and ready, they keep the little test tubes full of seminal essences from every encounter they've ever had. Charles James has got your ears, or so everyone no doubt keeps telling you. But I can't recognize anything of me in little *Banquet*. It's got its mother's eyes, that's the only likeness I can perceive. I mean it doesn't blink, whatever horrors are occurring.

And horrors keep occurring – far more horrors than ever before. Here we sit in Windy Ways, with the cows mooing just beyond the rhododendrons – and there in our book are aircraft tumbling out of the sky, a dog eating half an old-age pensioner, a girl raped on a runaway

Underground train by a group of marauding Centaurs. This isn't *my* nose! These aren't *my* knees! Or perhaps they are. Perhaps this is what I'm like. Even you may get surprises from your little publication, of course, as time goes on. Charles James, in spite of his ears being so much like yours, may turn out to be a physicist rather than a Germanist. He may sell your complete Mörike to buy pedigree sheep – marry a rock star – fail to discriminate between a Cabernet Sauvignon and a Pinot Noir. And then, of course, you'll gaze mournfully into the depths of your Coonawarra and wonder why he has rejected all that you hold most precious. Why does he have such a thirst for revenge? How have you so hurt and failed him? But I've had all my surprises in life already. Because two weeks after our fat infant had been placed in my arms, peacefully sleeping, it was a bundle of hopes and prospects no longer. I'd read it to the end. I knew everything about it that there ever would be to know.

Of course, it's a wonderful book. I should have said that before. Strange and sombre and audacious. And I do realize that fiction is invented. In fact I've spent my entire career explaining to students that the inventedness of fiction is its sign and glory. But that doesn't mean it comes out of nowhere, made out of nothing. What inventors invent tells you *something* about the world they inhabit. What fantasists fantasize has *some* objective correlative, even if it's only in the inside of their own heads. Otherwise our job, yours and mine, is impossible. We have to be able to relate these figments to the figment-tree they came from in some kind of way. There's

nothing so wonderfully mysterious about fiction – we all
fictionalize. I fictionalize all the time. Don't I, dear?
She's nodding . . . But you know perfectly well she didn't
nod when I asked her that – you know I didn't ask her –
you know she's not even in the room with me. You can
see what this tiny invention is for, though. You can grasp
the picture of life here that I'm trying to build up, you
can feel the general sense of irritation it conveys. So
when I'm presented with ten pounds five ounces of raw
lights I have to ask myself: what is she trying to tell me
about our life behind the rhododendrons? What is she
trying to tell the rest of the world about it?

And maybe it's not such a wonderful book, after all. I say
this to you in absolute confidence. Think about it, though.
Here's someone living peacefully in the depths of the
countryside. One peaceful husband, peacefully employed,
and peacefully married to *her* rather than someone else. No
one throwing things down the stairs. Loudest noise the
blackbird outside the window, and the Kawasaki bringing
husband home from work. Nothing more violent to do than
murder the slugs. And when she goes up to her book-lined
study under the eaves, what does she write about? Not
blackbirds and slugs, of course – I understand that. But
people being raped on the Northern Line? A pair of
abandoned shoes left inside a cupboard – with a pair of
abandoned feet inside them? Homeless Naiads living in the
sewers? And all this, of course, going on up in bloody
London! Don't you feel there's something just a shade . . . I
don't know . . . *inauthentic* about it all? Don't you think she's
pushing it a bit? Overcompensating for the blackbirds?

And if it's all genuine then I can't help feeling just a little piqued that she never mentioned any of these strange black holes inside her to me before she announced them to the world at large. How would you feel if you found your wife standing on the roof and shouting through a megaphone to the whole of Melbourne about bizarre horrors and miseries which she'd never so much as hinted at to you in private? Then again, I know that the middle-aged woman in the book who becomes involved in a coven of witches is not my dear old maj, nor anything like her. But will anyone else? *I* know that the rather feeble young man whom she kidnaps, then ties up, strips and rapes at a kind of feminist black mass, is not me, nor even any symbolic representation of me. But will the casual reader know? Will my colleagues? Will Swoff? Will Vlad? Will *you*?

What's happened to all that great drama on the stairs? I thought that's what she was writing about. I mean when I rushed up and tackled the madwoman. When I made her the Ovaltine. Why has she forgotten all about *that*?

I lift my head from this page for a moment and watch you reading it. I see that terrible right eyebrow of yours, which has scythed down greater men than me, once again upraised to strike. Yes, yes, yes – I realize I'm not being quite rational about this. I am aware that there are dark shapes stirring in the depths inside me as well as inside her, which you can see from up there on the bank more clearly than I can down here. One of them, of course, is simple jealousy. But I can see *that* great black carp for myself. All right – I'm jealous. Naturally. She's fecund; I'm not. I'd have to be half-witted not to be jealous. Though actually I'm *not* jealous, now I come to think about it. That's the odd thing. I rejoice for her – I rejoice with her. I just wish there were a little more to rejoice about. I'm aware of a few unfulfilled longings, certainly. Some of them brought on by your terse communication. I should have liked a little Charles James of my own, I admit, grown from my seed and no one else's, romping round my feet as I write, or doing his O-levels, or whatever charming reassurance your son is now giving you. That's beside the point, though. But I can't help feeling what a wonderful writer she was until I came along. This is what *Banquet* is telling me, while Charles James gurgles happily up at you – that I've grabbed hold of a delicate and beautiful machine, like a child taking its father's watch, and somehow ruined it. So now the watch is striking thirteen . . . fifteen . . . twenty-three . . . seventy . . . going on and on like a burglar-alarm instead of a watch, making some kind of accusation. To me and to all the world. Well, accusation and self-exculpation, counter-accusation and counter-exculpation – I suppose this is the basic mode of communication between married couples. Don't you find? We have taken each other by the hand, and led each other to the promised garden – a wilderness, as it turns out, of severed feet and half-eaten pensioners. Naturally we round on each other indignantly. No doubt you and D do too; or will do soon enough. But you do it in private! Not in editions of tens of thousands in hardback, followed by hundreds of thousands in paperback, plus promotion in North America and translation into Japanese. Of course, what's sauce for the gander ought to be sauce for the goose, and if she can chop me up for sushi in Japan, and mince me to fill hamburgers in Missouri, then I have every right to tell a handful of students and fellow-specialists that I feel one or two reservations about *her*. And she wouldn't even know I'd done it. She has never, in all the time I've known her, read a single word I have written about her – and it's not as if I've faced her with ten lb five oz on the subject to get through. Even so I can't do it. I can't stand up at the lectern and tell the world my wife's latest book is *inauthentic*! That's why I'm writing to you after all this time. I have my professional pride. I have to put my true feelings on record somewhere, even if it's only on a piece of paper which is then wrapped up and taken twelve thousand miles away, to be read by one single soul who will never reveal the contents to anyone.

So I haven't said any of this to her, then? Not directly. Have I, my sweetheart? She's shaking her head. But she's not a fool – she knows. Don't you, my precious?

She's nodding bashfully. Only of course she isn't. She's shut away upstairs under the eaves, doing heaven knows what. She's gone into a bit of a post-natal depression, to tell you the truth. Has yours? But then you probably feel unmixed critical enthusiasm for your little publication. You haven't had to sit for long hours over the supper-table trying to find formulations which didn't include the word 'inauthentic', while she discreetly tried to change the subject.

THE TRICK OF IT

I know what she's thinking. She can see my reservations about this book spreading slowly back to the earlier
ones – then soaking up through them until they reach the
author herself. She sees herself fading in my estimation
from majwoot to minwoot – perhaps from majwife to
minwife. Which just goes to show how little people
understand about literary criticism if they never read it.
The whole point of it is to discriminate. Though of
course that pair of spare feet at the bottom of the
wardrobe does in fact seem a bit like a parody of the dead
mouse in the teapot in *TBAD*, or the famous bloodstains
on the tablecloth in *WW*. But there was nothing forced
or arbitary about those earlier touches of the grotesque.
Or was there? And then suddenly I can't help thinking
that there's something a bit arbitrary, a bit sudden, about
her. Marrying me, for example. Walking out on her life
in London and moving up here. Wasn't that a little
improvised? Out of nowhere? Not properly prepared and
worked towards in the earlier chapters? A bit like jumping
out of the train in some station whose name you don't
even know?

What *is* she doing up in her study, in point of fact?
She can't still be working, because she's finished the
damned thing. Is she just gazing mournfully out of the
window? Writing to some old friend about how difficult
I'm being? My God – she can't be starting another one!
Already? I've always hoped that we'd have more books
eventually, of course. But there is such a thing as family
planning! She needs to get her strength back first – I
need to get *my* strength back.

Banquet still needs a lot of attention, for one thing. I say it's finished – but do one's parental responsibilities ever end? I'm going through it again at the moment, like a good father, marking all kinds of suggestions in the margin. I'm struggling to overcome my natural diffidence because I feel that this is one way in which I really can help instead of hinder – that I can put any slight negative feelings I have to positive use. I'm so close to her work – I know considerably more about it than she does. I'm also rather more passionately committed to it than she is. So I am simply the only person in the world who can assist with little *Banquet*, whether I'm the father or not. I long to hold out my arms to it and help it walk, help it speak and read and do its French homework. I'm full of ideas – I'm proposing a whole new section, in fact, in which she steps into the picture herself, as it were, and makes some kind of ironic comment on the sheer number of loose feet and electrocuted domestic pets there are littering these pages. This is what would help our strange little infant with his problems – some sense of detachment, of ironic self-awareness.

My God, though! When she sees quite how much red ink there is over her typescript she's going to retreat to her room for a month. Here she comes. I can hear her on the stairs. She's stopped . . . No, she's going back . . . What's happening? Hold on.

It wasn't her at all. It was my mother wandering around the house. We've got her with us, on top of everything. Not my idea. Her Majesty went over to see her last week, and found her very confused, gazing out of the window (a trait they have in common), with no food in the house. So she simply bundled her up like a parcel, put her in the car and brought her back. (She's learnt to drive. HM, not my mother – my mother can scarcely walk. That's another way in which her life has changed, and changed her in the process. It's also why I'm back on the Kawasaki.) This, it seemed to me, was a rather remarkable thing to do. Remarkably decisive. Remarkably generous. Remarkably vexing. Another of her suddennesses. Zig – marries me. Zag – rescues my mother. Where next? I was going to say it was as arbitrary as the sudden appearance of a lot of Centaurs clattering down the escalator at Waterloo. But perhaps it wasn't so arbitrary. It's just possible, I suppose, that she was repaying my silent reservations about *Banquet* with a silent accusation of neglect. She's been careering all over West Yorkshire and Devon this spring, like some maniac with a metal-detector, digging forgotten old aunts and half-cousins of mine out of the earth. I just hope she's not going to bring any more trophies home. I've got to get my mother into some suitable museum first.

I produced a little something of my own this summer, as a matter of fact. A paper. A paperkin. Forgotten now what it was about, it was so diminutive. No, I remember perfectly well – it was about nine pages. In the *Journal of English Studies*. Maybe you saw it? No, of course you didn't. I'll perhaps send you a copy.

I think, on mature reflection, that I got a little carried away when I described *Banquet* as *inauthentic*. That's a rather terrible thing to say – particularly in this case, since it's entirely untrue. In fact I regard the book as being among my wife's highest achievements, and am proud if I had any hand in making it what it is.

So to hell with me.

WHY DIDN'T YOU WRITE TO SAY YOU WERE coming? (Remember writing? All those clever little blue marks you used to make on bits of paper when you were younger to impress your elders, and defend yourself against me?) What a strange man you are! If you'd *written*, instead of creeping back into the country like abdicated royalty, and trying to astonish me with a surprise telephone call from ten miles down the road, we should have arranged receptions and dinner-parties for you, and introduced you to fascinating local characters like the Pope and Popess, and the lovely Popette. You wouldn't have had to make do with just us and 1s. and my mother. If we'd known you were coming we'd have baked a complete social and intellectual context for you.

Anyway, it *was* astonishing to see you again. Well, not so astonishing, really – rather astonishingly unastonishing, to tell you the truth. Moving, though, and disconcerting, and reassuring, and somehow rather irritating. Yes, I did in fact for some reason feel *irritated* the whole time you were here. Partly, I suppose, at being taken by surprise, without the chance to prepare a successful life for you to see. But also because you kept grinning all the time. And then again because I kept grinning. And because of what we were grinning at, which was not each other, but your bloody infant. It was like a kind of inverted tutorial, with the teacher sitting at the feet of the pupils, and keeping them all spellbound by saying nothing, while the pupils do all the thinking and talking for him. I'm going to adopt the same system in my own classes. I'm going to sit on the floor of the lecture-room silently bashing a plastic duck against the lectern while my pupils gaze at me reverently and say, 'Oh, look at him! "Take that!" he says. "You nasty bad Mr Twollope!" Oh, how sweet – he's thinking: "Can't you see I b'lieve in the cwitical function of the fictive act?" He's going: "I want my pension, and I want it now!"'

No, we both thought Charles was an inspired contribution to the human race. My wife, with her professional powers of expression and range of vocabulary, said it for both of us. 'He's wonderful,' she said, if you remember, not once but many times. 'Isn't he wonderful? He's so wonderful!' etc. This is of course what people always say about *her*, so it was a particularly striking tribute. I was too diffident to express my own more technical analysis at the time, which was that he is a fully achieved example of the babymaker's craft, effortlessly exploiting all the conceptual possibilities of the form. We both also very much took to D. I know my wife didn't pick her up and bounce her on her knee, as she did Charles. But this, she

explained privately to me afterwards, is because D seemed
such a fragile little creature. So beautiful, so delicate –
tinier than Charles, was my impression. My wife liked
you, too, I must report. The reason she didn't pick you
up and bounce you was the opposite one – she was too
awed by your size and substance. So, I may say, was I. Is
that the result of domesticity and contentment? Or is it
just the Coonawarra? Anyway, we discussed you all very
fully after you'd gone, and my wife, who as you know has
little critical discrimination, gave enthusiastic reviews to
all three of you.

In fact this was the other irritating thing about your
visit. We discussed you at such length that we couldn't
remember where we'd got to with the row we were
having before you arrived. I say 'row', but that's a word
for newspaper headlines and television comedies. It
doesn't do justice to the complexity of the negotiations
and manoeuvrings in which we were engaged, and which
extended over such a vast theatre that after you had
distracted us we could neither of us quite remember
where the minefields were, or which side Bulgaria had
been on, or what secrets we were guarding, or who was
winning. Did you realize you were walking through a
theatre of war? Holding up important hostilities, like a
family of tourists camping all unawares in the middle of
No Man's Land?

So we had to start the whole war all over again, and of
course we couldn't remember even what the starting
point was. If indeed we'd ever known. What's any war
about? Volumes can be written (and no doubt will be

about this conflict). In any case, this wasn't even anything as definite as a war. The question of what it was about, in fact, was so far as I recall one of the issues at stake. Was it because I didn't like her book? (This is what she believes I believe.) Or was it because *she* doesn't like her book? (Which is what I believe I believe.)

The truth is that her confidence in *Banquet* began to drain away while I was still reading it – long before I said anything about it to her. I would be reading the typescript, and I would suddenly realize that she had come quietly downstairs from her study in the middle of the working day, to stand looking out of the window or at the floor in some odd way – a way that maddeningly indicated how very careful she was being not to look at me and see how I was enjoying it. At which I, of course, would make my face more carefully expressionless than ever, and also lose my place and read the next page without taking anything in. Then she would disappear upstairs in a marked manner, and stay there for even longer than usual, to indicate that I was reading in some hurtful way. In fact I was reading it with great admiration and pleasure – I remember writing to tell you so at the time. When I finished reading, and told her how much I had admired and enjoyed it, she wouldn't look at me. She thanked me for taking so much trouble, etc., etc. She knew it wasn't my sort of book, and so on and so forth. The more reassuring I was, the stiffer and more awkward she became.

I was amazed by all this; I'd never seen her behave in such a way. For as long as I had known her, apart from

THE TRICK OF IT

the day of the Battle on the Stairs, and a month or two of gloom when she lost the previous book, she had been confident, decisive and untroubled. But then ever since the miscarriage she had been writing this book. She had been walking the parapets in her sleep, and now for the first time she was awake. She saw what a remote part of the roof she had got herself on to, and how precipitous were the drops on every hand. But when I showed her the queries I'd marked in the margins, and mentioned the ideas I'd had for improvements, she found reasons for dismissing them all in turn. A refusal even to consider sympathetic and constructive criticism, it seems to me, is a terrible vote of no confidence in oneself. But I persisted. I had to, for the sake of the book – for *her* sake. She conceded a few minor points of emphasis and simplification, a few piffling points of syntax. I conceded almost everything else in exchange for her accepting my principal point – that the book needed some strong central framework of ironic self-awareness to make its extravagance acceptable. She wept. (She actually wept!) I was firm. She said the book had taken her more than two years to write. I said all the more reason for taking another four weeks to rescue it. She said it was her book, not mine. I said that was why I was arguing with her. She threatened to abandon it completely. I threatened to let her. She retired to her study for several days, then came down with a new section in which an authorial figure of some kind emerges from her study and comes downstairs to confront the mayhem she has created. She asked if this was what I had meant. I said the question was if it was what *she* had meant. She said I seemed to know what she meant better than she did, etc. etc. I said this was a refusal to take responsibility for own actions, etc. etc.

It was somewhere in the middle of this huge barren plain that we were skirmishing when you and your exquisite Franco-Thai wife and jovial Australian son came wandering across the landscape. Which of course distracted us from the problems in our lives by uniting us in agreeable speculation about the problems in yours. In fact it's conceivable that the war might never have got going again if another army hadn't marched over the horizon at that point and pitched blindly in. Since you were here she has heard from her agent and publisher. And of course they love it. They think it's the best thing she has ever done, and, I am sincerely pleased to report, have no reservations at all.

Well, they have *one*. They neither of them like the bit where the authorial figure emerges from her study and comes downstairs.

You laugh. I laughed myself, of course. *She* laughed – a rare event. I plainly had to withdraw. Three to one against, and what was my opinion worth against theirs? I'm not a writer – I'm not a publisher – I'm not even an agent. I'm merely a poor dull scholar who happens to have devoted his life to the study and explication of her works. I also just happen to be right, though. A graceless thing to be; I apologize for it. There are very few things I am certain of in this world, but I *know* that this book will never work without an ironic framework to distance it, and if her agent and publisher don't like the small corner of a framework she has now provided it's because she wrote it half-heartedly, and sent it on to them separately, as if it were an afterthought. Which of course it was, but all the more reason for not allowing it to look like one.

The other thing that's wrong with the new framework, of course, is that there's simply not enough of it. The answer is not to give up but to press on – to provide lots and lots more of what they don't like until they learn to like it. And I am not going to withdraw gracefully. I am going to stand my ground. I'm not trying to restrict her, or make this book more like the others. On the contrary – I am trying to free her from herself, and help her to hold the new ground she is trying to capture. Without a strong controlling principle her spontaneity and invention run away with her. They did in her life. Not something I could have told you at the time, but she used to wear the most random collections of clothes before I took the matter in hand – cast-off flannel trousers, layers of vari-coloured woollies, underclothes that appeared to have been bought at different stalls in a church jumble sale. It's the same in her work. You know how passionately I admire her earlier books. Not one of them, though, that wouldn't be improved by a little more analysis and organization, by some really clear hard thinking about where they're going and what they're trying to do. So I'm fighting. Fighting her agent and publisher. Fighting her.

I have to give her the confidence to go forward. And I have to do it by shaking her confidence in where she is standing now. That's the paradox which, as we both know, is inherent in every teacher's task, in every critic's role.

Now a sudden doubt begins to assail *me*.

I am right in thinking so highly of her earlier books, aren't I? You've read them. (At least, I assume you've read them.) I haven't simply been deluding myself all these years, have I? A terrible question to ask. I can feel the earth move under my feet. But some hard-faced young market-analyst isn't just about to jump out of nowhere with a massive re-evaluation, which is going to leave all us shareholders with portfolios full of waste paper?

I'm sorry. I'm using up my stocks of confidence replenishing hers.

I'll tell you another irony. I'm losing my sense of irony as I try to develop one in her. You couldn't have guessed, as we all sat here grinning at your son, how seriously I take life now. Well, you couldn't have guessed anything. What with your great duck-thumping son lolloping at our feet, and our poor problem child locked away in the attic, we didn't manage to talk to each other at all. I've had better conversations with my fictitious version of you in one of these letters.

And now you're back in Melbourne. By the time you come again you'll have four children. I shall be too busy looking over my wife's shoulder as she writes even to speak to you. Damn, damn.

Life! That's what makes life so impossible.

FIRST THE GOOD NEWS: DR SPOFF LIKES IT. DR
Spoff (who is not a real woman, of course, but a
humorous personification of the Society for the Propaga-
tion of Feminist Fiction) thinks that *Banquet* is (and I
quote the letter from the publishers which brought the
glad tidings) 'an astonishing new milestone in the development of the author's fiction . . . the keystone that ac-
complishes and locks the arch of her achievement . . .' A
milestone, you see, and yet at the same time a keystone.
What other critic could put it with such compelling
grace? But how, you will ask, has an unpublished manuscript fallen into the hands of a critic? Even more to the
point, how did the particular pair of critical hands in
question come to belong to the great Dr Sloff? (The
name, interestingly, is derived from a small town in the
western Ukraine, presumably where her forebears came
from, which is noted mainly for its provincialism and its
low-grade brown coal.) Presumably the publisher sent it
to her. Geoff. This is how he signs himself. A name that

inspires little more confidence than Snoff. In fact they
sound like a pair of music-hall comedians, or extracts
from some old-fashioned north country dialect novel. –
*Ge' off, tha girt boggart! – Sn' off thasen, tha grungy hali-
but!*

You will ask why Our Geoff should interrupt his
simple knockabout routines to airfreight ten lb five oz of
unpublished fiction across the Atlantic behind his
author's back – why this honest clown should be seeking
the opinion of some consultant in Arkansas when we
already have the opinions, copiously and freely given, of
a full-time resident consultant here – me. The answer is
simple. Oor Geoff and JL's agent (whose name, even
more unpromisingly, is Sam, which suggests to my ears
not a literary agent but a trade-name for sliced ham) are
trying to come between husband and wife. They are
struggling to persuade the wife to abandon the small
improvements she has made to the book at her husband's
suggestion. These consist of a series of ironic personal
interventions by the author in four different parts of the
manuscript, transforming it (in my humble opinion) from
an interesting genre-piece into a potentially major work
of art, and adding no more than half an ounce at most to
its overall weight. (I say potentially because I feel – and
she on the whole agrees – that we need at least another
seven similar sections elsewhere in the text to complete
the transformation.) Wee Geoff says nothing in his letter
about the four new sections, of course, and nor does Dr
Smoff (not a Slavonic name, surprisingly, but an Anglo-
Saxon one, derived from *smoev*, a form of laxative por-

ridge) – which is how I know he has not shown her the latest draft. Because if he had she would have joined the general outcry against the sections. With her limited and stilted powers of response she would have liked them no more than the Chairman of the Group, and the Managing Director of the Children's Book Division, and the woman who works the copying-machine, and all the various other distinguished authorities they have dragged˙ in to put pressure on J L.

I make light of it, but these parasites are in fact subjecting J L to the most intolerable strain, and if I were not here to advise her and strengthen her resolve I think she might easily give way. They are destroying her confidence, that's the worst thing. She keeps appearing from her study clutching hesitant drafts of the new sections, and asking me what I think about them. She has never asked my opinion of a draft before. What I think, of course, is that she should write what *she* thinks. I'm not trying to *impose* something on her – which is what Giff, Poff and Spam, our lovable farmyard friends, are trying to persuade her – I merely want to help her to locate the true shape and nature of the book, to discover what is still hidden inside herself. But when I say this she sulks; retreats to the garden and starts digging and hacking at things; then abandons that, ostentatiously crumples up the abandoned draft, refuses my offers to talk about it and shuts herself away in the study for several hours. I'm really quite worried about her. I can't help feeling that if I weren't here to watch over her all the time they'd come and get at her here – and next week

I *shan't* be, because term starts and I shall be out of the house all day. I'm sure you worry about Charles – but at least you don't feel that everyone in the world, from the paediatrician to the local postman, is trying to persuade his mother to pour poison down his throat every time you turn your back. Well, I *assume* the manuscript was sent to Oklahoma behind J L's back. I *assume* she is not secretly conniving in an appeal to an authority for whom, as she well knows, I feel a particular professional contempt. All the rest of the crew's baled out; maybe the pilot's slipped silently off the flight deck as well, and I'm the only person left aboard to get the stricken jumbo down.

Sorry. I'm becoming slightly obsessed. None of this can be of much interest to you. It's just that when you can actually see the answer to a problem, and apparently no one else can – when your entire life and work have enabled you to help bring something of true transcendent perfection into this imperfect world . . .

Sorry, sorry. I'm really writing to thank you for your letter. I was very touched by your offer. Yes, by all means let me know if you hear of a job going in Australia. I don't think I'd succumb, but it would be nice to be tempted. I suppose we did look rather pale and peaky beside you two, and I'm sure you're right that we could do with a little more sunlight in our lives. You're too tactful to put it in so many words, but you're correct in your implication that my career here is somewhat becalmed. I assume I'll be renewed, but it would take an outbreak of botulism at some annual conference of university English specialists before I had any realistic prospects of promotion in this country. And JL, as you say, could work anywhere. Then again I have to confess that the sight of you, all fat and contented, with your tiny wife and fat, contented baby, had an unsettling effect on both of us. Perhaps this is one of the reasons we are getting in quite such a state with each other over our own pudgy, sun-starved child – why I am quite so determined he will become prime minister and justify both of us. And yet . . .

And yet one does get quite attached to one's own pigsty, you know. These grey skies and chill winds; these dreadful dormers; these bonfires smoking sullenly at the bottom of the garden; these long silences while she works; this great muddy battlefield that stretches around us from horizon to horizon – it's home. I bought a car when we moved here, to get to work in, and slowly, painfully learned to drive it; and how do I get to work? On my motorcycle still. Why? Because I've got used to it. Because I know where all the puddles are on rainy mornings. Because I know how to slip inside the queue of cars at the lights by the hospital, and then outside the queue for the right turn on Dirac Drive. Because I've found a place in the boiler room that no one else knows about to hang my wet leathers up. Because I've grown to like it.

I don't think I could uproot JL again, in any case. She's forty-eight next year, which is a bit late in life to change hemispheres. Once *Banquet* is out of the way she'll presumably be struggling to start the next one.

Easy to lose the baby, as you know, in those first few months. By the time she's really got into her stride, though, she certainly won't want to be interrupted. And then, if I know her obstinate, dogged nature, she'll want to keep her head down until she's finished. By which time, of course, she'll be in her fifties – and starting the process all over again. My one gift to her in this life has been the stability and peace she needs to work. Which is to say that nothing has happened, nothing is happening now and nothing will ever happen again. Not if I can help it. No lovers, no Japanese autograph-hunters on the doorstep. I go through the mail. I am deeply discouraging on the telephone. I have built a cork-lined life around her.

Her only distraction is my family. I don't know why she finds them so interesting. They seem to me about as dull as a family can get. I feel rather uneasy; all these old pots and pans at the back of the cupboard, and suddenly here's some grand antique-dealer wanting to look at them. It's become a ritual; I don't see her giving it up to go to Australia. She suddenly tells me on Sunday morning that we're having tea with my Auntie Annie in Sowerby, or Ted and June and Mrs Naylor and Bill whatever-his-name is and his sister Viv in Hebden Bridge – although none of that lot are really family at all, I don't know where we picked them up. I complain, and sulk, and make us late. She drives – I read the map wrong – we get even later. But when we arrive of course we have to pack up the war and put on a bit of a show, as we did with you (though of course it didn't fool you). And it's all very jolly; my relations are proud of me, because I've got on, and I'm proud of them, when it comes down to it, because they haven't. They've never heard of her, of course. I've told them she writes books, but they didn't take it too seriously – they can see she's just one of them. So Auntie Annie puts her hand on JL's arm (which she never does on mine), and tells her about laying her mother out and washing her ('I used carbolic soap, my love. For the germs, you see. And that's where I went wrong, because you could smell her halfway down the stairs'). Ted and June go through the accounts of the shop with her, ice-cream by ice-cream. Viv whispers to her about Bill's prostate. And of course I'm tremendously bored. But in some weird way I enjoy it. This is a confession. I look at JL and Auntie Annie, and I feel curiously fond of them both. I think it reminds me of . . . Wait a moment, doctor, while I stretch out on the couch so I don't have to meet your eye . . . It reminds me of going out with my mother. Is this unnatural? Shameful? I don't know. All I know is that when JL and I drive back we're always in a good mood. And I never lose the way.

Her own family were solid professional people – I suppose that's what makes mine seem so picturesque in comparison. I can't say that the converse is true, though most of her lot are dead, which may take the shine off them a little. She has an older sister concealed in north London somewhere, who came to our wedding. She's a very forceful woman, who counsels people – much, I imagine, as a road-roller counsels roads. Her husband's in the Ministry of Defence, and she goes on anti-nuclear marches to demonstrate her independence of mind. She also traps people at wedding receptions and tells them the plots of Jane Austen's novels, and never reads anything by her sister. I have absolutely no desire whatsoever to take tea with her on a Sunday.

As a matter of fact J L and my mother became very close towards the end. My mother disapproved of her for a start, of course (you were the only friend of mine she ever showed some cautious enthusiasm for). You'd have thought one's parents might be reassured to have their child marry someone a little closer to their own age. But my mother wouldn't even come to the wedding reception. She took one look at J L in the registry office, and afterwards she wouldn't speak – wouldn't even take my arm to go down the steps. 'Oh, Richard' – that was all she said. 'Oh, Richard.' Then she got back into the car I'd hired for her, and wasn't seen again. J L won her over finally, though. She was the one who found her gazing out of the window with nothing to eat and brought her home to stay with us. She was the one who persuaded her to see the doctor. She was the one who coaxed her into the local hospital, and washed her nightdresses, and sat with her every afternoon while she was still conscious.

Did I tell you my mother had died? Last November. Secondaries in the bowel. Perhaps I didn't even tell you she had cancer.

Or how much I loved her.

I'm not sure I've even told you how much I love J L, for that matter. In spite of what you might think.

But then men don't talk about these things.

I'VE SUDDENLY DISCOVERED THE JOYS OF FREE-fall parachuting.

It was at one of the sessions the Pope has taken to holding in his office on Monday mornings to talk about the future of the Department. He was rambling on in his now familiar style to me and BD and Lynn Welsh about outreach to industry and a market-led approach to the arts, and I was just thinking, 'Poor old Lynn – this sounds like the final curtain for her dreadful Theatre and the Dynamic for Social Change course,' when it suddenly dawned on me that *I* was the one who was being brought in for a respray. 'A shift of emphasis from the literary to the visual narrative . . . a growing awareness of the financial implications of fiction . . . the development of communication skills . . .' When he got on to the challenge of cable and satellite television I thought I'd better save him from embarrassing us all further. 'Why don't you discuss these exciting new perspectives with whoever you appoint to teach the course?' I said, with heroic insouciance. 'Since my resignation will take effect before it begins?'

No great clamour, I'm afraid, greeted my announcement. No overwhelming demand was voiced by either management or staff for the resignation to be withdrawn. Lynn, I think, was too surprised that it was me and not her disappearing through the trapdoor. BD was gazing at the waste-paper basket, absorbed so far as I could tell in his problems with the Beldam. (Yes! Have I told you about this? Never mind, I will.) His Holiness himself inclined his head in silence, and raised his hands, as if gracefully submitting to a gunman. Polite surprise, I think this was intended to convey, together with acceptance and possibly also a parting benediction as I withdrew from the Papal presence. 'Oh,' he said, softly but with great significance, and the remark seemed to him so apt that he made it again – 'Oh.' And then he said it three times more, with a pause for reflection before each performance. 'Oh,' he said. 'Oh. Oh.'

So there I was, falling through the empty sky, with the plane dwindling in the distance. And what I felt was pure exhilaration. No more fastening of seatbelts! No more air-traffic delays! No more powdered coffee in plastic cups! You must try it some time. You're free and alone in all the huge blue emptiness. You can fling out your arms – no walls to bash them against. Hurl yourself head over heels – no floor to crash down on to. You can recline in the soft hammock of rushing air and feel the closeness of the sun. Then roll over and study the map of the world tens of thousands of feet below, wondering how long you can leave it before you need to open your parachute, and in which of those green meadows and yellow cornfields you're going to float to earth.

You may, it occurs to me, think I left the plane rather precipitately. A routine announcement from the captain about diverting to a slightly different destination, and I was out of the door, taking the quick way home. But this was only the last of a long series of hints that I was going to be bumped off the flight sooner or later. In any case it's J L they're getting at, not me. That's why I felt such an intoxicatingly generous rush of indignation. The Pope and his supporters in the Holy Office have been trying to get her off the syllabus for a long time, though they've never had the courage to say so to my face. The insinuation used to be that the students weren't interested in her books any more. This was a downright lie. Plenty of students have complained to me about every other author on the syllabus, from Ariosto to Ed McBain. Not one, though – not *one* – who has ever come up to me and said, 'I don't see why I should have to read your wife's books.' They *like* them, in so far as they like anything. *TBAD*, one of them told me only last week, was 'quite a chunky number'.

In fact what the Holy Father and his unholy crew object to is really neither her nor me. It's the combination. It's husband expounding his own wife. They've never dared say it to me – and I suspect they can't even formulate to themselves what's worrying them – but from the very beginning, from the very day I came into the Faculty Dining Room and saw HH giving me one of

his looks over the soup, they've felt some strange primi-
tive distaste, some obscure disgust as for the prospect of
kid seethed in its mother's milk. It's never been a difficulty for my students because it's never been a difficulty
for me. At some point in the first term with each new
class I've been aware that the word was going round once
again. I've just stared all their unasked questions down,
and gone on saying what I've always said – I'm still
using the notes I lectured from before I met her! I
happen to know now why she was so obsessed with the
idea of twins when she wrote WW – but I don't embarrass my students with personal revelations, whatever
some other members of the Department may suppose. I
stick with the precise set of reservations and limiting
judgements I had before I knew her. Not by one jot or
tittle have I reduced or softened them; nor, by the same
token, have I seen any professional necessity to share
with them any doubts I may have had since. I know
what's brought the Curia's discontent to the boil now. It
used to be her supposed unpopularity; now it's exactly
the opposite! It's because they've made *Scatterbrain* into
a television series. You'd have thought this was precisely
what they wanted – market-led, popular communication
– with commercials! – for all I know piped through cables
and bounced off satellites. But in a funny way it's too
highbrow to be lowbrow, and too lowbrow to be highbrow. Huge numbers of people are watching it. Including
a lot of the students. Even the Holy Mother, I happen to
know. It's terrible, incidentally.

So there I am, falling down the empty sky. That's

why I'm writing. To say PLEASE SEND PARA-
CHUTE. Because it occurred to me only when I finally
reached to open it that I had omitted before leaving the
plane to provide myself with this obvious and elementary
requisite for the sport.

Let me put metaphor aside, and say it in raw plain
English: I need a job. You wrote in I think the last letter
but one that you'd let me know about the chances of a
job in Australia. Did you by any chance happen to notice
one lying around? You didn't mention it in your last
letter, but perhaps this was because I didn't have the
prescience to take you up on it earlier. It wouldn't have
to be in Sydney or Melbourne. Or even Adelaide or
Perth. I'd be happy to float down to earth in some quite
small place, if that's where the work was. Some little
sheep-shearing town in the middle of the bush would do
me fine. Anywhere they might like to hear about the
narrative tradition from the *Mabinogion* to Magic Real-
ism. Or the non-narrative tradition . . . Or the changing
significance of sheep in the pastoral poetry of the late
eighteenth century . . . Or how to write television
scripts . . .

In short, I'll do anything. Except live off my wife.
Living in her house for the last four years has been bad
enough. I've told her I'm looking for work abroad. She
didn't raise any objection. In fact she didn't say anything
at all, just went on repairing the vacuum-cleaner. Later I
realized she was walking round the garden in a rather
marked manner, looking thoughtfully at the plants. But
she could perfectly well make another garden. Don't

worry about her work — she can work anywhere. As long as she's got her head with her, that's all she needs.

In fact she could work a lot better in the middle of the outback, because she'd have a bit more peace. Since this television idiocy started all my efforts at shutting the world out have gone for nothing. I've only succeeded up to now, I realize, because she hasn't had anything published since I've known her. Now suddenly the world has rediscovered her, and she's happy to talk to all of them — reporters, television researchers, charities, housewives who've written historical novels. She invites them down if I don't watch her. We've had two complete television crews here this year. I come back from the university and find the drive blocked with vans and estate cars. I go inside, and I can't make the dinner because the kitchen's full of exhausted young women with English degrees, and disenchanted electricians with beer bellies. I can't sit down or work — or even watch television, ironically enough — because all the furniture's been moved around. I can't *see* anything, because the house is full of blinding light. And there she sits, in chairs she never normally sits in, wearing clothes she never normally wears, screwing up her eyes, and getting more and more miserable because she hasn't been able to work all day. The press are worse. They don't move the furniture round — they describe it, and me along with it, if I don't move fast. I'm her 'craggy egghead husband number two', according to one of the titsheets, with what a litsheet identified as 'a boyish grin'. They love my being ten, fourteen or seventeen years younger than her, whichever they happen to decide it is. They love even more my lecturing on her; I've already thrown 2, 5 or 7.4 reporters out of my classes this year. Presumably some of this might be avoided if we lived in the remoter parts of New South Wales. Though as a matter of fact some Australian paper sneaked in a few weeks ago while I was doing the weekly shop. I don't suppose you read it, or you might have been surprised to find that I didn't exist at all. I was rather pleased, I have to confess, by this sudden existential lightness. That was *my* problem solved, anyway. The cornfields and meadows were rushing up towards me, and I had simply abstracted myself from the situation – woken, as one does from a dream of falling.

In any case I might just as well not exist as far as she is concerned. I think I told you I made a number of very careful and sympathetic suggestions about her book. Well, I now discover that she has adopted none of them. Not that she bothered to inform me. As far as I knew, she was still sitting in her study considering them. In fact I'd rather forgotten the book, with all this great uprush of air past my ears. I was standing in the hall one morning putting on my leathers, absorbed in my own grievances, when the postman arrived with a bulging package from her publishers. The proofs. Even while she had been going through the motions of listening to my criticisms, tramping down the stairs with half-hearted redrafts to show me, then tramping back again and tearing them up, Ge' Off and his merry men had been setting the original manuscript. She'd been performing a fiction for my benefit. I thought about this during the day, with growing indignation, and put it to her, politely but forcefully, that evening. She looked evasively out of the window. She is a profoundly evasive person, I have discovered. She offered a few devious explanations and hints about making the changes in proof. She is a very devious person, too. This is another discovery I have made about her. She looks so simple and straightforward – but she retreats into fantasy just as she retreats into that study of hers. It would do her good to emerge from her own inventions for a bit and look at the world around her. She could start on the wallabies and billabongs. What *has* she been doing in that study all these months, I wonder.

I *wasn't* pleased, in fact, to see that cutting from the Australian paper. I was profoundly irritated. It happened to be the day after the proofs arrived. Here was I, expected to bend and bow, to give up teaching her books and adapt myself to studying horror comics, or else hurl myself out of the plane with no chance to check if I had a parachute, while she coasted along without listening to anyone. Here was I, falling into nothingness, already forgotten about, while she sailed along in first class with her headset on. And I'd had to be about four times as clever as her to get on to the flight in the first place!

I'm sorry. Slightly tense moment, though, in all our lives. That green-and-yellow counterpane is getting very close. I can see now – it's not meadows and cornfields at all. It's swamps and stony desert. 'May,' I am increasingly inclined to murmur, 'day.'

I'VE FOUND THE ANSWER TO ONE OF LIFE'S riddles, anyway – I now know what it is she's been doing up there in her study every day for the past four months. I was slightly mortified that I had to get on to it by chance, in the course of making small talk with her agent on the phone while I was waiting for her to come in from the garden to take the call. 'How's it going, anyway?' asked her agent, the famous Sam, in the sliced-ham-like tone of voice she adopts for talking to university lecturers. 'Oh, fine,' I lied, assuming, ridiculously, that she was referring to something connected with me. My work, perhaps. My career. My life. Things. The indefinable *it* whose going is usually inquired about on these occasions. 'Fine,' I assured her a second time, to make it more true. 'That's jolly good news,' said Sam, who has to be convincingly chummy with all the variously unsuitable consorts her clients choose for themselves, 'because she's being awfully mysterious about it with me.'

This is when I realized we were not aboard the same

135

train. We were on parallel tracks, gazing through the glass at each other, only a few feet apart, as if sharing a compartment. But a gap was opening up between us. How did I know that it was not my work, my career, my life, my *it* that my wife was being so mysterious with her agent about? I just did – I just happen to have enough self-knowledge to know that people don't go round being mysterious about me. The only thing I didn't know was where her agent's train was heading. 'What?' I said. Some faint inkling came to her at this point, I think, that I was about to veer off the main line. 'What?' she said, uncertainly. (Do you have this kind of conversation in Australia, too?) 'I'm sorry,' I told her frankly, 'I don't think I know what we're talking about.' 'This new thing of hers,' she said. 'This whatever-it-is that she's written the first something-or-other of.' 'Oh, that,' I said. 'Yes, yes.' And of course she realized that my train was stopping short at some small suburban station, while I realized that she was disappearing over the horizon aboard the non-stop Pullman.

So, my wife had written the first something-or-other of a new whatever-it-was. As one of the country's leading specialists in her works (until the end of the current academic year, at any rate) I was naturally pleased to know this. After nine novels and a collection of short stories she was adventuring into the uncharted waters of the whatever-it-was. What did she feel about the possibilities of this exciting new form? Our interviewer took up the question with her over dinner:

INTERVIEWER: I believe I'm right in saying that you've finished the first something-or-other of a new whatever-it-is?

JL: Sorry?

INT: Or do I mean the first whatever-it-is of a new something-or-other? Sam was telling me on the phone this morning. She asked how it was going. I gave a somewhat guarded reply. I hope that was right.

JL: Oh, that. That's just something I'm trying to . . . I don't know . . . Something.

INT: I see. Thank you.

JL: There's no need for that tone of voice. I'm not keeping anything from you. I don't know what it is yet. I don't know whether I can do it. I don't really know quite what it is I'm trying to do.

INT: So it's not a novel?

JL: Oh, no. At least, I don't think so.

INT: You don't *think* so? Come on – you know what a novel is. If you don't know what this is then it can't be a novel. You also know what a short story is, since you've written twenty-seven of them. So I think we can conclude it's not a short story. That's two possibilities excluded. I believe we may find out what this thing is, in fact, by a simple process of elimination. It could be helpful to you, couldn't it, if we could back it into a corner and identify it?

JL: I don't understand. What's all this about?

INT: I'm using my analytical and critical powers to help the creative process. Can we also assume, on the same grounds, that this thing you're writing is not a play, or a film, or an epic poem, or a television commercial? In fact, since you know what fiction is, we can eliminate all forms of fiction. So it's non-fiction. It is some attempt to come to grips with the world outside your own imagination. My God – it's not *literary criticism?* No, I can see from that absolutely spontaneous curl of the lip that it's not literary criticism. What are we left with? Biography?

JL: You've been looking on my desk, have you?

INT: Certainly not. So it's biography.

JL: It's not biography. It's not even remotely biography.

INT: Non-biography, then. Non-biography of whom, I wonder. Not of *me*, by any chance?

(*There was a pause in the interrogation here, while the prisoner gazed obstinately down at the bare interview-room table, and the interrogator rocked his chair back on its heels and gazed at the prisoner, waiting patiently.*)

JL: No.

INT: Not me?

JL: No. I'm trying to write something about your mother.

And there you have it. She is trying to write something about my mother. She is wrestling with literary form, struggling (as she went on to explain) to find some simple, direct way of recording the bare facts of my mother's birth, life and death; of her appearance and character; of her thoughts and feelings; of marking her passage through the world. The book (if we can assume for the moment that the whatever-it-is will at least have pages and a jacket with a price on the front flap) may reach out to take in other members of my family as well. Auntie Annie in Sowerby, for example, and Ted and June and Mrs Naylor in Hebden Bridge. Everyone she's met, in fact. Even possibly Bill and his sister Viv, who are not in actual fact related to us. Every single one of the tribe. Except me.

I'm naturally delighted. Delighted that Auntie Annie is going to be suitably memorialized. Delighted that poor Ted and June, after a lifetime's drudgery in that terrible little shop, are going to be vivisected for literary experiment. Particularly delighted that J L has got some reward for nursing my mother in her last illness. My poor mother, I suspect, would probably have left her something in her will, if only she'd had something to leave. It would probably have been a great comfort to her to know that she was in fact bequeathing her entire life.

And maybe my mother *should* have a book written about her. Why not, after all? She was worth no less than all the other people who get books written about them. My only regret is that J L has so abruptly lost her taste for the ludic possibilities of fiction, when some of us have committed our lives to them. All I question are these increasingly erratic changes of direction. I wondered, as you know, about her sudden swerve into abandoned feet. But if you're into abandoned feet, it seems to me, you can't just veer wildly off again into abandoned aunts. As a critic – as a reader – one does want to know what a writer's up to, where he or she is off to next. One looks for consistency and organic growth, not drunken driving.

At least, I assume we're not going to find my Auntie Annie's house filling up with severed limbs and mutilated animals. I assume she is going to spare us *that*.

Then again, I have to confess to a certain pique that I have not been found edible myself. My entire family lies

gasping on the bank, waiting to be gutted and filleted
and turned into delicious fish-stew, while I'm tossed
back into the river.

No, on the whole I was delighted. So delighted, in
fact, that the very next day I wrote to accept a job in the
University of Abu Dhabi. Did I mention I'd applied?
Probably not; it was just one of a whole series of random
mail-shots I've fired off in the last few months, each wilder
than the last. Oh, that's what I should have said at the
beginning of this letter, not forty-eight pages later: thank
you! I mean for taking so much trouble over that job in
Cairns. I should have jumped at it, of course, if I hadn't
already jumped in the direction of the Persian Gulf. Still,
it's a good thing from the point of view of her research –
much easier to drive over to Sowerby from the Persian
Gulf than from Queensland.

In fact it will be ideal for her. Long days uninterrupted
by telephone calls from agents or admirers. (Do you
know she is not published in Arabic? I checked.) Shutters
over the windows, nothing to be heard but the hypnotic
hum of the air-conditioner. Perfect conditions for writing.

I am even going to be writing myself in those empty
Arabian afternoons. Have indeed put a few preparatory
words down on paper already. This in absolute confidence; I haven't told her yet. But it's one of the many
complex reasons why I decided to settle for Abu Dhabi.

I believe I see that right eyebrow of yours sardonically
deployed. I believe I sense, about three inches behind
the eyebrow, a tiny surge of jealousy and panic.

Is this the long-awaited study of narrative from Gilgamesh to *The Golden Bowl*? you ask. No, it isn't. A rather unpleasant suspicion strikes you. It's not the long-awaited critical study of *her*? You plainly know little about me if you think I would use my reverence for her work to score some kind of personal point. – It's not by any chance a somewhat less awaited study of her mother? – I shall not even trouble to answer such a ridiculous suggestion.

I'll give you a clue. This letter, it occurs to me, is a kind of simple first attempt at the form I am working towards. The dialogue between myself and J L so meticulously recorded above, for instance. You must have wondered as you read it. How was I able to reproduce it so fully? Had I made a shorthand note at the time? Did I have a tape-recorder concealed beneath the kitchen table? The suspicion must have come to you, as someone in the literary business, that I was giving my recollections a little extra substance and definition.

You still haven't grasped, though, how radical my treatment of the problem was. I didn't improve on things: I just made the whole damn thing up from start to finish. We never had any such conversation. The entire dialogue is a kind of metaphor for the rather complex events that actually occurred – the process of guess and counter-guess, of glimpses over her shoulder when I took her cups of coffee she hadn't asked for, of silences and frowns, of looks and glances, of an accusatory tilt of the jaw here, a defensive set to the mouth there.

Your expression changes. You are beginning to feel, I

do believe, some slight embarrassment on my behalf. Exactly. Fiction. Just when she is trying to find her way out of it, I am trying to find my way into it.

I don't mean, do I (and here your voice goes down a tone and a half), that I am . . . *writing a novel*? So what if I am? What's wrong with writing a novel?

I mean, come on. Never – not once in all my thirty-seven years – have I given way before. I know you've got some shameful, seedy manuscript hidden away some-where down there in Melbourne, though you've never had the courage to admit it to me. This may be my last chance before I die, and I'm not going to be put off by the sight of a few faint mocking smiles on the other side of the world. Nor by the fact that *she* happens to be occupying the fortress already. In fact it was she who put it into my mind to try. The flaws in her new book, that I can see and no one else can – they suddenly seemed to me to offer a way through and under the mighty ramparts of literature. It came to me that I could squeeze my way through those unremarked cracks and take the fortress from within. Watching her at work, in any case, has rather radicalized me. I don't see why the great castle of fiction should remain the exclusive preserve of the privi-leged few. I don't see why it shouldn't be made over to the National Trust, and thrown open to the populace at large. It's a trade, writing, that anyone can learn, not a Masonic mystery. Part of my aim is to demonstrate that any bloody fool can do it.

I haven't said anything about this to her, of course – her sympathy and encouragement would be even more difficult to bear than your ill-concealed scorn. I'm not going to say anything more about it to you, for that matter, since you've taken it the way you have. Well, I'll tell you the kind of book it's *not* going to be, to save you from making a few misplaced gibes. It's not going to be the kind of book where the central character is teaching English at a provincial university. It's not going to be about a man marrying a writer, or a younger man marrying an older woman. Nor will it be about a younger woman marrying an older man, or a civil servant marrying a designer of fairground steam-organs. In fact it's not about me at all, or any stand-in for me. I can write it now because I've got the experience in life – the experience to know that it's not this experience I'm writing about.

Not, you note, that I've agreed it *is* a novel. It may be. It may not be. I don't know. It's a whatever-it-is. It's a something-or-other. She's not the only one who's licensed to hunt literary forms. It's going to be very strange, I can tell you that. And deep. Let me just mention the square root of minus one, shimmering back and forth between negative and positive throughout all eternity; and unseen people laughing in the mist on November evenings; and the summer of 1654; and exultation; and that bridge we sat on by the old cardboard-box factory.

An impressive list? Well, not one of those things will be in the book. What's in the book will be stranger and deeper still.

I'll tell you something else about it, though. It will be good. It may be very good.

I believe I can see how it's done. That's what's changed. I believe I can see the trick.

Just possibly, if it proves too difficult to check on the citizens of Sowerby from the remoteness of the Persian Gulf, *she* will end up lecturing about *my* work.

S O HERE WE ARE, BASKING BENEATH THE BLAZING
Abu Dhabi postmark.

I'm sorry for the long summer of silence, but you can
imagine what desperate packings filled our lives, what
desperate unpackings again to retrieve things prematurely
packed, what form-fillings and cupboard-emptyings, what
rendings of the heart, what rentings of the house, what
injections and dejections, what forwardings and backward-
ings, what helpful briefings, what unhelpful longings,
what second thoughts and first impressions.

Anyway, now we are beginning to come out of shock,
and to discover that here is where we are, and have been
for some time, and evermore shall be. And the first thing
you will want to know is – what's it like?

I will tell you what it's like in one colourful paragraph.

It's like an air-conditioned, viewless, well-sound-proofed
office halfway down a long empty corridor in a largely
uninhabited new concrete building; this quiet retreat
shared with a tall, thin man from Omaha, Nebraska,

who has tall, thin religious beliefs, and teaches English Drama 1500–1970.

This tall, thin man (will you believe the wild tale from Araby I am about to unfold?) regards Dr Szoff both as the world's greatest authority on fiction, and also as one of the only two conversational resources we have in common. The other one is his good friend Vladimir, in Chicago. Vladimir is Professor Katc, more familiar to you and me and the rest of the civilized world as Vlad the Impaler. Actually this *is* an Arab story, it occurs to me – it's the one about the bloke who meets Death in Damascus and flees to Samarra, not knowing that all he will achieve by it is to provide John O'Hara with the title for a book. But the cost of fate these days in terms of precious jet fuel! It's had to bring me and my tall, thin portent from Omaha (who does look strikingly like Death, now I come to think about it) an aggregate of some eleven thousand miles to reach our fearful appointment here.

No, I'm carping. Half my life, after all, I spend not in my air-conditioned, viewless, well-soundproofed office at all, but in my air-conditioned, viewless, well-soundproofed apartment, which I share with a much more congenial colleague. Relations between J L and me (I can now confess to you) were becoming a little tense back home, and the move here has cleared the air. I think getting her away from my family has helped. Also the fact that I'm working on a book myself. (Did I tell you I'd started something that may or may not be a work of fiction? I see a sardonic eyebrow lift off the launchpad down there in Melbourne . . . Oh, yes, I did tell you.) So instead of spending the evenings fretting in the living room, feeling abandoned, I'm softly clicking away at the electronics in the spare bedroom. While *she* frets in the living room. No, no, she usually works in the evenings, too. Parcelling up my family. I've even become resigned to that. I rather welcome it. I like to think of her sitting in her room with her head full of Auntie Annie, while I sit on the other side of the wall with my head full of . . . whatever it is full of. A mystery, which shall be revealed unto you in due course. You are going to be rather surprised, I think. I'm surprised already. I felt in England that I'd come up against the edges of myself in every direction. Now here I am, outside my old life, outside myself, on my way to the Thirty Years War in one direction and Alpha Centauri in the other. And I'll tell you the great secret I've discovered: anyone can do it, even me. It's like making love, or all the other things that look so fearful until you actually try them. It's like free-fall parachuting. *How* do you do it? You just do it. You step out of the plane, that's all, and there you are, doing it.

To be absolutely honest I like it here, in spite of my tall, thin friend. It's so clean. I mean clean of people, clean of all their tedious talk. They don't have agents here, or publishers, or television researchers. No old friend of hers with space to fill in a failing literary magazine lives within three thousand miles of this place; no film producer has yet realized there are telephones here; organizers of petitions probably have their hands

cut off. All those bluebottles buzzing in one's ear –
'Would she could she might she . . . speak write read
judge sign stand come go . . . consider decide review
advise . . .' have faded to the soothing hum of the air-
conditioner.

Not even the publication of her book disturbed that
beguiling soft murmur. The day came; nothing happened;
the day went. A few reviews began to arrive, as thin and
unreal as the airmail paper they were printed on. They
were full of praise, but the shouting was in another
street. She read them; I read them; the air-conditioner
hummed. 'Good,' I would say. 'Very good. Well done.
Congratulations.' Mmmmmmmmmm, said the air-conditioner judicially. She would tap her teaspoon against her
cup, or look, from force of habit, at the view out of the
window, which was of course of the inside of the shutters,
and say nothing at all. None of the reviewers seemed to
have noticed anything amiss about the book. None of
them seemed to think it should have had some kind of
ironic framework. I was no more disgruntled by this than
she was gratified. Perhaps I had been wrong. Perhaps
there had been nothing wrong with it after all. Perhaps it
is the perfect book, as perfect as only far-off things can
be.

I've just realized, as I describe to you our life here,
what it is I like most of all about it. That it's a fiction. A
fiction written in an unfamiliar language of concrete and
chilled air – and a fiction written by someone else. This
is its great charm. We are living in someone else's house
and sitting on someone else's furniture. We are ruled by

someone else's government, which someone else has to reform or remove or endure. We are breathing someone else's air. No wonder I feel free here. No wonder I can write my own fiction. I have, after all, given my life to the study of this strange intoxicant, and have at last been pickled in it, the way drinkers in songs hope to end up pickled in alcohol. I have been taken up, like a desert father after a lifetime's contemplation of God, to become one with the object of my devotion.

Oh yes. My tall, thin friend tells me that someone is collecting J L's letters. Not the mighty Vladimir, as we all supposed – it was Vladimir who told him – but some newcomer we have never heard of, some still unformed young pipsqueak scarcely out of graduate school, with one of those still unformed names, like Rhees, or Timmins, or Dubby. He is said to be writing a critical study of J L. Which of course is good news – the more the merrier – delighted to welcome a fresh challenger to the lists, etc. But why does he want her *letters*? You don't need letters to write a critical study. I think he has his sights on something biographical. Some fawning piece of PR done with the subject's consent, or else some piece of scandalmongering done without. Or perhaps he is putting his marker down for when the great standard life is commissioned in years to come.

Well, we've all got careers to carve. But I suppose he'll be trying to get his hand on *my* letters, too, since I'm part of the story. I assume you'd mention it if he approached you. I mean you'd *refuse*, of course. Wouldn't you? Perhaps you wouldn't. Perhaps I am addressing not just you but Mr Phelps and all posterity. I'd better start putting footnotes in, explaining who people are. You [1] do understand, don't you, that not everything I say is to be taken literally? I'm sure you do. You can read, can't you, between these somewhat inconsequential lines, all the good things I never mention, all the tenderness I have felt towards the subject of your researches, all the security I have given her? You can see that it was for her good as much as mine that I brought her out here. Too much contentment and gardening can undermine a writer. She needed shaking up. I presented her with the challenge of desert heat and sheep's eyes. *Plus* Christmas puddings sent out from Fortnum and Mason, and that softly murmuring air-conditioner. The best of both worlds. Shaken, but shaken gently. She loves it as much as I do. All right? Got that transcribed? This *is* the kind of thing you want to know, is it? You're not hoping to find out how often we make love? I know what you scholars are like.

You want me to what? Just carry on normally, as if you weren't there? Of course. Fine. So . . . Are you [2] well? And D? [3] And Charles? [4] (Can you [5] read my hand-writing, by the way? Not much use my carrying on normally if you don't know what I'm carrying on about.) Sorry. Where were we? Oh yes. So you're all well, are

[1] Mr Nobbs.
[2] Here: = you.
[3] Daniela – your wife.
[4] Your son.
[5] No, *you*, Mr Pipps! Wake up!

you? What's the weather like in Melbourne? M-e-l-b-o-
u-r-n-e. MELBOURNE. Well, I mustn't ramble on
forever, or I shall miss the post . . .

No, I know. I'll tell you about a small but significant
experience I had here the other day. It was something
that (I think) captured something of the heat and colour-
fulness of Abu Dhabi, but which also elicited in me a
rather important feeling about life, as these little incidents
tend to do in poems and letters written by people making
academic visits to exotic locations.

Picture, if you will, then, the empty, sunbaked street
at midday, as I drive back to our housing development
on the outskirts of town for lunch. I am at the wheel of
the small air-conditioned car that comes as part of the
job, with nothing to be seen through the green-tinted
windscreen but blinding white empty roadway, when
suddenly a little dusty motorcycle shoots out of nowhere
in front of my wheels. I brake – the motorcyclist swerves
wildly, loses his balance and goes down in a storm of
swirling jellaba. I scramble out of the car into the midday
furnace, already seeing the casualty ward – the morgue –
the prison where I am awaiting execution. The motorcyclist picks himself out of the dust, though, plainly alive
but extremely voluble. He is pointing at the roadway, a
widening area of which is now no longer dusty white, but
dark and gleaming. Blood! No, not blood, because he is
not bleeding – he is indicating, forcibly, the emptiness of
a large, open tin-can, labelled in English 'Snow Queen
powdered-milk substitute – catering pack', which he had
been cradling like a son in front of him as he rode,

shaded in the folds of his jellaba. Powdered-milk substitute? Can powdered-milk substitute be dark and wet and gleaming?

A small crowd appears out of the noonday emptiness. We all stand around in the hard iron heat, I hopelessly gesturing apology, they gazing at the gleaming patch in the road as if it were a television screen, eagerly discussing (I assume) its appearance and provenance, and lamenting its fate. And suddenly I understand. I have spilt something more precious than blood or powdered-milk substitute. I have spilt *water*.

This little incident, I think, makes a succinct and colourful point about the importance and preciousness of water in a desert economy. But to me it suggested something else as well. Because by the time the crowd had dispersed, and the motorcyclist had dusted himself down, the wet patch on the road had ceased to exist. In those few minutes under the noonday sun it had lost first its gloss and then its dark wetness. It had become nothing but a faintly coastlined whiteness in the whiteness all around. And suddenly I thought, that's not just a story about water. That's a story about me. I could disappear off the face of the earth here just as easily, and leave as little trace behind.

We both could. I told J L about the incident over lunch, and explained the feelings it had elicited. She looked thoughtful. I think the story could be used, in an otherwise rather under-documented section of some future biography, to suggest, albeit obliquely, her state of mind at the time.

Our life here is a pure fiction, as precious and evanescent as water. That's my point.

Got that, Boggs?

No, but seriously, I should be grateful to be reassured that my letters are still safely filed away inside that ant-proof steel filing-cabinet down there.

Y OU DIDN'T ANSWER MY QUESTION. FIVE FASCI-
nating pages about Charles's amusing difficulties pronoun-
cing the word 'Mörike' and the amusing hugeness of your
wife's belly – for all of which news I of course thank you –
but not a syllable about whether you have been approached by Mr Fillis. Perhaps you didn't realize that
my question was serious. Perhaps I got the name wrong
– it's a name which is very easy to get wrong. Or perhaps
you have already given him my letters — sold him them
– I hope you stood out for a good price – and dare not
mention it. Perhaps you are trying to distract me with
these twelve pages about the little comedies of family life.

Let me say in so many words that I am writing this in
a humorous tone of voice. Some people apparently find it
difficult to tell. If the humour sounds a little edgy it's
because I'm a shade sensitive about unanswered questions
just at the moment. You see, I don't believe it was news
to JL that Mr Fillis was writing this so-called critical
study. I believe she knew about it already. I believe she

authorized it. I put this to her, in a humorous tone of voice, and she declined to answer. She declined to answer, she said, on principle. What principle is that? I asked, humorously. Her right to conduct her professional life as she saw fit, she said. Didn't she realize, I asked, no less humorously, that I was asking in a humorous tone of voice? No, she didn't, she said. Well, I was, I assured her. So, she replied, it wasn't a serious question? Yes, I confirmed, it was a very serious question indeed – it was a serious question asked in a humorous tone of voice.

At this point she gave up all pretence of arguing reasonably.

'You own the questions,' she said, 'but you don't own the answers.'

It was yesterday evening when she made this rather strange pronouncement. We were standing in the entrance hall of the house – I was just about to go back to the university to give an evening lecture. The hall is nine feet long by five feet wide, so we were very close to each other, and there was no room to move about, or gesture, or shout. She was speaking very quietly. I imagine I was smiling.

'Your professional life is a matter of some professional interest to *me*,' I said, as lightly as before. '*Your* professional life is *my* professional life, if you recall.'

She began to speak very oddly. We had spoken very little for several weeks, and she may have got out of practice. She spoke very levelly and seriously, which is not how married couples normally speak to each other, and in curiously literary phrases. 'You have led me into a desolate and stony place,' she said, 'and things are very bad between us. You hedge me about, you cage me and patrol me, and take all the ground and air from around me. But you don't own the words I say or the thoughts I think, and you never will, and you never can.'

I'm not absolutely certain she said 'hedge me about', if the exact words are important for the record. It may have been 'fence me in', or 'mew me up'. I realized that an important declaration was being made, but there was no chance to take a note, or rush for the tape-recorder. She was staring at me over the top of her spectacles without blinking, in the way she used to in our first months together. I could think of no reply, I regret to say. It didn't occur to me to ask her why she had agreed to come with me to this stony place, if she was so free, or why she stayed now she had discovered its desolation. If only she had put her foot down firmly enough, for that matter, I should never have come myself. But then I suppose the stoniness she was complaining about stretched well beyond the boundaries of the United Arab Emirates.

So I stood my ground and stared smilingly back at her. She went on gazing at me. She looked more sad than angry. I wondered whether to put my arms around her, but went on smiling instead. The air-conditioner murmured. There seemed to be no reason why this period of human history, with her gazing sadly at me and me smiling fixedly at her, should ever end. But then she sighed, and went into the kitchen. I continued on my way out through the front door and got into the car. I turned on the air-conditioner and sat there, unable to think where I was supposed to be going. My hands were shaking.

So you see I am not in the mood for unanswered questions at the moment. Being here is like one of those experiments in sensory deprivation you read about, where the subjects go mad and start to hallucinate. The whole familiar world is blotted out by sand and distance. I seize upon little snippets of information in the airmail editions and the literary journals – allusions to events I haven't heard about, incomprehensible jokes, strange unexplained names – and build great monsters from them. Fillis, for example. *Fillis!* There's no one in this whole wide world called Fillis! I invented him. I misread the name. I misunderstood the joke. Fillis . . . And is he writing a critical study or isn't he? Perhaps it's merely a critical article. A review. A shorter notice. Nothing.

No, I know what happened. He phoned her one day. He was a voice from home, a voice from the old life. And he sounded young and vulnerable – just starting out in his career – in need of a helping hand. She felt she couldn't say no. He was another of her sons. A Mark-III son. The first batch have fallen by the wayside (one of them's running a junk-stall, you know, the other's a meat-porter). Then the replacement she got for them (that's me) went on the blink. And now here was this nice young man on the line, bounced charmingly off a satellite at her, the way all the best narrative fiction is going to be in the future. Sons – that's what she wants. She thinks she knows how to get on with sons. This is why the husbands don't work out. The first one never was a son, that was what was wrong with him. The second one was, but then he grew up, and took a critical look at her and her work, and tried to collaborate with her as an equal. A terrible mistake.

Why does this Fillis man need authorization from her to write 'a critical study'? For the same reason that he needs to collect her letters, of course. The 'critical study' is going to grow, one way or another, into a biography, just as I knew it would. How does he know I'm not writing a biography myself? I'm the obvious candidate for the job, aren't I? If for no other job in the world. So who has told him I'm not doing it? Not me. Not you. That only leaves her. And then again, *if* I'm not, *why* aren't I? Doesn't he ever stop to ask himself that very simple question? Doesn't he see that I don't do it because a life of the living can't be done? Not a true life. Not without the grossest violation of the subject's feelings. And if he doesn't see, why doesn't he ring me up and ask me? Why is he nervous of getting in touch with *me*?

Or perhaps he's not going to do a life of the living. Perhaps he's just circling overhead, waiting for her to die. Then he's going to be all ready to swoop. I don't suppose it will worry him overmuch if I'm still alive. I'll get eaten along with the rest like all the other worms in the carrion. Before I can write a truthful memoir of my own I shall have been pilloried and discredited in advance.

And if I'm not very careful most of the material is going to come out of my own letters! That's what hurts.

Look, has he approached you or hasn't he? I must know. I must have a definite answer. You may be able to reassure me; I may be suffering quite needless anxiety. But whether he has or whether he hasn't I want you to do something for me. A small and simple thing. I want you to destroy all my letters.

Do I sound a little mad? I am, I am. When I think of that first night in the guest room . . . When I think of running insanely into town to send her the flowers – of walking up and down the street outside her door, willing her to come out – of putting my arm around her the day that woman smashed up her house, of making her Ovaltine and feeding it to her in a spoon, of all the love and goodness between us, of how happy we were . . . well, then, yes – I *am* mad. I am, I am.

That's why I want those letters destroyed. To protect *her*. To stop her from being seen at moments when she was unseen by anyone but me, when she was undefended. I don't want to be used as a keyhole for peeping in at her.

To protect me, too, though. I don't want people thinking I've used her just to write myself into the record, to give myself some foothold in existence by becoming part of her history.

In fact I want those letters destroyed for both our sakes. It's a chance to expunge our lives. Our lives are not what we meant, not what we meant at all. This is our chance to unlive them, to strike them from the record.

The only memorial to my life on this earth is going to be my book. How can I write it in the midst of all this, though? I sit at my desk, and I'm deafened by the air-conditioner. All I can think about is how my life – and hers, and hers! – is being stolen by someone who understands nothing about either of us. While on the other side of the wall she works on, apparently unaffected. Writing about my family, without any reference to me. But they're changing, my poor family, out here in the heat. They're growing *stories*, like mouldy bread growing fur. She's finding explanations for the way they are and the things they did. She's giving them pasts she never knew, inner lives she could never observe.

And don't think I'm creeping into her room like a spy, snuffling through her papers. I don't need to. I know it from looking at her. Because I know *her* inner life all right. I watch her across the table every day and I know every thought that's passing through her head. That's why the idea of Mr Fillis writing about her makes me laugh. If only he knew what I know he'd laugh at himself.

She's *naming* my mother in there. I felt a flash of pure shame when I saw that, as if I'd opened a door and caught my mother naked. Her first name – her surname. She spares us nothing. I won't repeat them – I don't want to embarrass myself further. Why am I so shy about proper names? For a good old structuralist reason. Because they are uniquely arbitrary signs. They could be anything. Fillis could be Figgis could be Figgin could be Biggin could be Mewle. They are fictions. Their naked gratuitousness is not cloaked by common usage. Their harsh particularity is not softened by generalization. I admire the ancient Israelites, who had seven names for God and uttered none of them. I remember telling you once (I'm sure you've forgotten) about my sister, who died at the age of four. I didn't tell you her name. I've never uttered it to my mother, either, nor she to me. And the word 'father', following immediately after the word 'my', I still find difficult even to think.

Listen, this is my mother, as captured on the famous hundred-gram Conqueror bond: 'She goes fearfully to the window, and looks fearfully out, pressing her fingers to her lips; sits down at the table once more; goes fearfully back to the window; again and again, like a small, nervous, stiff-legged grey bird moving back and forth between a crumb of bread and flight.'

When I read that I felt as if my mother was alive again and moving back and forth in front of me, in all her old anguish. It was as shameful as hearing her named. Why should people have the right to exhume the dead like this? To expose them to view? To start pain and recognition in the living?

Like a small, nervous, stiff-legged grey bird . . . I may have misquoted. I'm relying on memory, not a photocopier. And then she was *inside* my mother. She knows *why* my mother keeps going to the window. 'She thinks she can hear footsteps over the noise of the traffic and the children playing. She hopes they might be her son's; knows they are not; believes they may be news of him; fears it is bad news. But there is nothing to be seen; only the children playing and the traffic passing, only the weather and the wind, only God and his universe; nothing.'

Sons again, you see. And such nonsense. Her Omniscient Majesty doesn't know what went on inside my mother's head. Her guess is no better than mine, which is that it wasn't fear for me she was holding in with those four thin fingers pressed against her lips — it was some nebulous nameless dread she couldn't even have identified herself. Why should anyone have the right to break into my mother and steal me away from her? To break into me, and steal my mother away from me? 'She thinks she can hear footsteps . . .' What evidence, what application, could those words have now except the guilty sense of recognition they might arouse in me? A recognition which I most certainly don't feel. All I feel is that I wish I hadn't read them.

Two pages further on she was not only inside the house but opening the safe — she was back into my mother's past. Back to a winter's night when my mother was nineteen, nearly twenty years before I was born, when she was a pretty girl running home from work through the fog 'with the corner of her blue scarf held over her mouth, and November diamonds sparkling in her hair'. And suddenly the tears came to my eyes. It was the blueness of the scarf that did it. So stupid. There never was such a scarf, or such a night. They were made-up things. And yet somehow I was glad to find my mother young again, running along the street, with a home to run to, and a blue scarf, and the droplets of fog trembling in her hair. Was it my mother I was weeping for, or the words? It was the way the words caught her, the way they honoured her, like sunlight haloing and honouring a cloud.

162

So I *was* creeping into the great queen's room, then, and looking at the papers on her desk? Once. Only once. In desperation, because I was slightly mad, from the mad struggles I was having next door, trying to write my own book, hurling words and more words down on to the paper, and hitting nothing, *naming* nothing. I wasn't trying to find out what she was doing – I knew what she was doing. I just didn't know how she was doing it. After all these years I still had not the slightest idea how the conjuring trick was done. And this time I'd seen the whole performance going on right in front of my eyes – that's what maddened me. In slow motion. Month by month, nothing hidden. It wasn't like the novels, where probably it was all done with secret wires to her childhood and concealed tubes to her unconscious. I'd seen the aunts and mothers put in – I'd seen the words taken out. So simple!

But how had the one turned into the other? I was trying to find some bit of apparatus that might give it away – notes, drafts – I didn't know what. I found notes, I found drafts. And of course they explained nothing, just as I'd known they wouldn't. I may be mad, but I'm not a fool.

I've been watching her for more than four years, and I've seen everything. But the essential bit – the gadget that makes it all work, the crystal, the chip, the formula, the dodge, the wheeze, the scam, the flick of the wrist, the twist of the fingers, the whatever it is – *that* remains as invisible as the peacocks' tongues at her banquet.

So I only looked the once. Once was enough for me to

catch myself up. And then of course she was out only once. The rest of the time she's been in there. Working – that's all she knows how to do, poor love.

Do you know where I'd like to be at the moment? It's just come to me with great force. I'd like to be walking along Dirac Drive, looking at the back of Machine Intelligence. I used to think it was the dullest road and the ugliest building in all creation. I was wrong.

Don't worry about me. I'm only mad in private, talking to you. The rest of the time I'm as calm as an air-conditioner. I'm still teaching her, of course. I think they were hoping for Dickens and Galsworthy, but what they're getting is her. As always. That's where I was going last night, as a matter of fact, when I was held up by our great confrontation in the hall. That's what I was going out to do, once my head had cleared a little and my hands had stopped shaking – I was going to give an evening class, and tell some ridiculous group of diplomatic wives about the devices she uses for distancing the narrative in *TBAD*.

So don't worry. Just burn the letters – and send me the ashes. Put all thought of the photocopier out of your mind, incidentally. You see how suspicious I'm getting. But, truly, if you even think of photocopying them first I shall *know*, and God will know, and one or the other of us will strike you dead.

And make *particularly* sure this letter goes up with the rest. What's in the others I can't remember – probably nothing so very damaging – but Fillis could obviously have a field-day with this one.

So – BY RETURN – AIR FREIGHT – IN A CASKET – THE ASHES OF MY LIFE!

Oh, I should have said earlier – best wishes. It must be due any day now.

Aм I THE ONLY MAN LEFT ALIVE? HAVE THESE blinding deserts and shimmering salt seas reached out and devoured the old green world beyond? I've phoned you five times. Nothing. No one. I've cabled you twice. No reply but the huge silent roar of the air-conditioner. So here I am reduced to sending another letter hurrying off through the wilderness, trying impossibly to overtake the letter I wrote yesterday. Who knows, perhaps the first one is still lying unopened on your doormat. Or perhaps by some freak of the postal weather this one will catch up, and come galloping out of the distance just in time, nostrils wide and flanks foaming, thundering into the prison-yard even as the rifles are raised, shouting:

DON'T!

destroy the letters.

I asked you to destroy all my letters to you. Don't.

Don't.

I thought about it all night. Walked up and down the living room, sat at my desk, dozed in an armchair. It all came fizzing up inside my head like some monstrous Alka-Seltzer. Then it settled again, until around six a.m. the contents of my head were as flat and calm as a glass of water. I turned off the air-conditioner and opened the shutters. The whole world was as still as I was. The air was almost cool. Out over the desert in the west the sky was translucent grey, as gentle as purring pigeons; out over the Gulf in the east the most discreet lemon, the most intimate pink. I stood there waiting for the sun to rise, and I suddenly realized that I had the four fingers of my right hand pressed against my mouth, just like my mother in JL's book. The only difference was that the sunrise I was waiting for was impersonal and inevitable, a mere wordplay on the rare and private sonrise for which she was longing. Words and echoes of words; this was all I had. I understood quite plainly as I stood there what I couldn't understand yesterday, in the hugeness of my indignation. A sad and simple thing. That those letters to you are all that remains of my life.

I've lost her, I know that. She's in there working now, but great deserts and empty seas lie between us. She's as desolate as I am, I know. Or she would be, if she didn't have the book. That's why she's so obsessed with it. Because it's not the great hot here – it's rainy England. Because it's a world where I am not, a world I have vacated, a world I am not to be allowed even to survey. That's one of the things she said that night. 'I won't be told where I'm allowed to go. I won't be told what I'm allowed to think. I won't be made to defend myself for going where I go and doing what I do.'

And that's connected with another thing. She's never accepted what *I* do; she's always despised my trade. Well, for a start I think she was amused that I wrote and lectured about her works, was even slightly flattered, though she never read a word of what I wrote. But the amusement settled into contempt, and the flattery into distaste. And when she spurned my trade she spurned me. What else did I have in the world? What was I but that?

Now even that's gone. My job here is unskilled labour. I might have fought harder not to lose my old employment if she hadn't so devalued it.

I suppose that's why I started the book. To have something. To have something that even she might recognize as something. Did I tell you I was writing a book? Strike it from the record, if I did, because it's no longer true. I put it out in the dustbin during the night.

Actually it never was true. I discovered this at about 3.15 a.m. One of the skills of my late trade, which I haven't yet forgotten, is to distinguish between a novel and a stack of waste paper. This particular specimen, I discovered to my surprise and amusement, when I actually read it through, was an example of the latter. I hadn't worked on it for some weeks, in any case. How could I? To write a book you have to be obsessive. You have to be prepared to destroy everything around you. As she is. As I am not. This is another thing I discovered about myself as I stood at the window, breathing the slightly cooler air off the Gulf and watching the sun come up: I am sane. I may be a fool, but I'm not mad.

I've touched fire and been burnt by it. Burnt out of house and home. Stripped and skinned by the flames. But not consumed. Not quite.

I was a cocky little fellow, wasn't I? I don't feel so cocky any more.

The only thing that keeps her here, I think, is the book. She has to finish it before she can look for another life. This is her madness. When the fit passes she will go.

Quite funny, really. She's abandoning me for my mother. Perhaps this will ensure me a foothold in the world's footnotes.

So all that remains of my life is the letters. As long as the letters exist I have a past and a present, and a trace of all the happiness that my old maj and I had together will remain. I want you to take photocopies of them and send them to me. Take two photocopies – take three. Put them in different places, so that they can't all be washed away in the same flood or hit by the same thunderbolt. I'll take copies of the copies you send to me, and put them in safes and bank vaults. Something of me is going to survive.

I've just rung your number yet again. Teatime in Melbourne, and still no answer. So it looks as if this letter really is my only chance to deliver the reprieve. I'll get it to you in time somehow. I'll air-freight it – I'll fax it – I'll charter a private jet. From the depths of my new-found sanity I feel insanely certain it will arrive in time to save my life. All will be well.

Let the record stand. Let my life stand, let all our lives stand. This is the message of my serenity. Why should we start crossing ourselves out and rewriting? What we are is all we have.

So stet. Stet.

The phone. It's you. I *know* it . . .

Yes. Well. Twenty-five minutes have gone by since I wrote the last paragraph. The first five of them, after I put the phone down, I spent gazing blankly at the blank wall in front of me, unable to think or feel anything. The last twenty I have spent walking up and down my room making such insane noises that my future ex-wife even broke off her labours in the next-door room to come and investigate. I think she thought I was having a heart attack, or some kind of gross psychotic breakdown. 'What is it?' she demanded, irritated at the interruption. I shook my head helplessly. I couldn't explain. I couldn't even stop laughing. When she realized that these terrible gasps and groans represented mirth she went away again, even more irritated. Laughter is not her mode, poor love.

Because it *was* you on the phone. Precisely as I foretold. Or almost precisely. It was your words but not your voice; your cable, read over to me by the local operator.

'Letters lost.' I shall remember that brief alliterative phrase as long as I live.

Human destiny, in two words. It really is perfect. I sit up all night in the agony of my soul, trying to decide whether to burn my life or not – and then I find there's no life there to burn. It's been put in the wrong folder – thrown out with the old newspapers – eaten by dingos. I suppose it's gone for good. I've suddenly dissolved. I've become as invisible as other people's thoughts. But then possibly it hasn't gone for good. Just as the courts finally agree to presume it dead, it will turn up again, like some embarrassing ne'er-do-well relative. In bits, probably, wrapped round someone's grandmother's crystal goblets. Or in Mr Fillis's burgeoning files. Who knows? Not you, evidently. Not me. No one. My life is in the hands of God, just where religion teaches us it is.

'Letters lost.' It really is a wonderful opening sentence. And when I'd at last stopped laughing at that I started all over again at the next sentence: 'So no problem.' And then again at the last sentence: 'Frederick Lescott Pendle George born one p.m., seven lb seven oz.' So that's where you were when I was trying to phone you. How ironical. Having dropped the remains of my life down the back of the radiator you were at the hospital bringing the next one into the world. Don't file poor little Frederick Lescott Pendle George away with your old lecture notes, will you. You can be filed away yourself for that kind of mistake.

Well, congratulations. You're down there extending human life into the future; J L's next door extending it back into the past; I've scarcely got a hold of any life at all, even mine, even here and now.

It's like that Arab's can of water. You balance your life hugely and awkwardly in front of you as you go along. It seems so important – you can't think of anything else. Then suddenly some stranger comes bowling down the street – someone who hasn't even seen this huge and secret load you're carrying. You lose your balance – and there's your life in the road, already disappearing in the sun.

Though rather more of a crowd than I've managed to attract gathered to watch that water evaporate.

Anyway, I'd better post this latest instalment off. Scatter the pages in the wind when you've read them – give them a sporting chance.